Critical Acclaim

"Chip Hughes has captured the semi-hardboiled vernacular of the classic gumshoe novel, and given us an authentic Hawai'i, believable surfing scenes, good pidgin, and realistic local characters. Like a session in smooth blue water." *Ka Palapala Po'okela Excellence in Literature Award*

Murder on Moloka'i
"Hughes's pastiche of hard-boiled noir and the zen goofiness of surfing bliss is effortless and entertaining." *Honolulu Star-Bulletin*

Wipeout!
"Just right for the flight to the islands. Hughes's prose flows easily, slipping into Hawaiian pidgin when needed. His series remind[s] readers of a charming new *Magnum, PI.*" *Library Journal*

Kula
"Zips right along . . . pacing is first-rate . . . dialogue is snappy . . . strikes a nice balance between the Hawaii of today and the film noir memes of yesterday." *Honolulu Star-Advertiser*

Murder at Volcano House
"Glides along at a satisfying clip. The landscape and characters are consistently colorful. Hughes effectively uses the native Hawaiian language throughout and provides vivid descriptions of the legendary island scenery. Entertaining Hawaiian whodunit." *Kirkus Review*

#5

HANGING TEN IN PARIS

Trilogy

Hanging Ten in Paris

Another Problem in Paris

Murder at Makapuʻu

Other Surfing Detective books by Chip Hughes

MURDER ON MOLOKAʻI

WIPEOUT! & HANGING TEN IN PARIS

KULA

MURDER AT VOLCANO HOUSE

*SURFING DETECTIVE DOUBLE FEATURE
VOLS. 1 & 2*

SLATE RIDGE PRESS

P.O. Box 1886

Kailua, HI 96734

slateridgepress@hawaii.rr.com
ISBN: 0999253808
ISBN-13: 9780999253809

Hanging Ten in Paris © Chip Hughes 2012
Back cover photo by Austin Clouse.

SURFING DETECTIVE

CONFIDENTIAL INVESTIGATIONS | ALL ISLANDS

HANGING TEN IN PARIS

Trilogy

CHIP HUGHES

SLATE RIDGE PRESS

For Miriam and Alan
who showed me a Paris I'd never seen before
and will never see again.

Acknowledgments

Many thanks once again to my wife Charlene for reading and commenting on *Hanging Ten in Paris Trilogy* and for being my partner on life's many journeys. To Stu Hilt, the generous, humble, and brilliant Honolulu private detective who has guided me through every Surfing Detective mystery, this one included. To Christine Matthews, for editing an early version of the first story, and to John Michener of Mediaspring. And to Deborah L. Ross, Laurie Tomchak, and Nathan Avallone for providing invaluable editorial advice. Special thanks to Lorna Hershinow for her superb copy-editing and for resetting the moral compass of both the PI and his creator. And to Cinda Inman for her eagle-eye proofreading. Finally, *mahalo* to Miriam Fuchs and Alan Holzman, without whom these Surfing Detective mysteries would not have been written.

Contents

Preface

I got the idea for "Hanging Ten in Paris," title story and Part I of this trilogy, when I was in Paris one autumn after the passing of my mother. Though I came to celebrate the birthday of a dear friend, my mood was understandably somber and I could not shake the dark omnipresence of death. In this atmosphere of sadness and gloom, one evening in a restaurant in the Latin Quarter near the Panthéon I observed a table of a dozen diners—all, except one, American students. The one exception was also an American, a man of at least twice their age. The man could only have been their professor, and their dining together a celebratory event during a study abroad term in Paris.

I knew this scene well because the year before I had taken such a group to study across the channel in London. My students all had come from University of Hawai'i, where I taught at the time, some having never before left the islands. As might be expected, a few had problems adjusting to a new culture and a very different climate—it was January when we arrived and spitting snow. My job was to help them adjust and to ensure that each returned to Hawai'i alive and well. All did, thankfully. But I had heard horror stories from previous terms.

Glancing at the dozen students dining together that evening in Paris, my perceptions still clouded by gloom, I began to imagine the worst: what if one of them turned up dead in some tragic and shocking way?

This bleak question followed me through my last days in Paris, until I finally tried to answer it in the form of a Surfing Detective mystery. Then I encountered a problem. Why would Kai Cooke investigate a death in Paris? He didn't speak French. He'd never been to France. And his normal sphere of operations was the six inhabited Hawaiian Islands. My PI was therefore an unlikely detective to take the case.

I was stuck. Until I saw two connections between him and the proposed victim: like Kai, Ryan Song would be from Hawai'i and he would be a surfer. Then I pieced together a scenario in which Kai would investigate Ryan's death some months later, upon the request of his parents. And due to the Songs' limited means, Kai would conduct his inquiry without ever leaving the islands. No trip to Paris. That meant a challenging case. How would the PI reconstruct a sequence of events that occurred months earlier and seven thousand miles away?

Another issue was length. From the beginning I had conceived the case of Ryan Song as a short story rather than a novel. This would mark, in fact, the first time I had attempted a Surfing Detective mystery in this compact form. Yet when I began to write, the case kept growing and growing—beyond the bounds of the short story, but not reaching the length of the novel, or even the novella. So what did I have—a long story? I was pleased to rediscover the term *novelette,* whose length is midway between the short story and novella.

The longer narratives that follow in Parts II and III—
"Another Problem in Paris" and "Murder at Makapu'u"—
were prompted by a return visit to the same friend who was
then herself teaching in Paris. I stayed at a university residence
among students and consequently was once again immersed
in the atmosphere of the earlier story.

I began to contemplate a new case in which Kai himself
would travel to Paris. But how and why? He still had only the
slightest knowledge of France and the French language. He
didn't even hold a passport. The scenario I finally imagined
picks up where "Hanging Ten" leaves off, carrying forward
key characters and events in the lingering shadow of Ryan
Song's dangling toes.

In "Another Problem in Paris" Kai flies to the city of love
with all expenses paid and an attractive guide with whom
he has a history, having been hired to deliver an envelope.
Upon his return to Honolulu he takes on another case set in
motion by the previous one. In "Murder at Makapu'u" Kai
investigates a fatal plunge from the cliffs on O'ahu's southern
coastline that looks suspiciously un-accidental.

Each of the cases in *Hanging Ten in Paris Trilogy* is linked
to the others and can be read together as one continuous
narrative in three parts.

Part I
Hanging Ten in Paris

"What the hell did you do?"

"Get out of my room!"he shouts.

They struggle, knocking over a small table, anger raging as they fall and he lands hard on the floor.

"I told you—we all told you to shut your fat face!"

He doesn't answer. He doesn't even move.

"Oh, my God! Is he dead?"

No use talking any more.

one

"It's Kai Cooke, the surfing detective." My arrival is announced by an assistant to Serena Wright, Director of International Studies at Paradise College in Honolulu.

"Quite sad about Ryan," Serena says as I take her hand. I stand almost a foot over her, but what she lacks in stature she makes up in intelligence. She's fortyish, British, and very bright. "I only wish we could put this behind us, Kai."

"The Songs are no doubt grieving," I say as I sit down across from her.

"That's not the problem," she says. "They don't believe Ryan killed himself. And they think that you—a surfer like Ryan and a private detective—can somehow prove he didn't. I tried to dissuade them, but it was no use."

"Thanks for the gig," I say.

"Your broad shoulders and sun-bleached hair should convince them you're the genuine article."

I almost say, *And the shark bite on my chest?* but simply reply, *"Mahalo."*

She opens a file drawer and hands me a sheet with color headshots of Ryan and his fellow students from the Paris program—four girls and three guys—seven in all. There is a name under each photo and contact information. Serena points to a handsome boy of about twenty with luminous eyes, short spiky hair, and a shy smile. His face is open and sunny.

"That's Ryan," she says.

"Looks like a nice, happy kid."

"He was quiet. I think that's why he fell for Marie. She's the life of the party." Serena points to an attractive island girl with bobbed hair, grey eyes, an intelligent brow, and a playful smile. She looks full of fun.

"Opposites attract," I say.

"Ryan was clever too. His French was the best in the group, next to Marie's, and he played the guitar and had a gorgeous voice. The girls adored him. They took his death very hard. Marie was devastated."

"And the guys?"

"I doubt it was much easier for them. Or for Russ . . . uh, Professor Van."

"What a shame," I say.

"If only Marie hadn't met that fellow Pierre in Paris . . . ." Serena fills me in, then opens her file drawer again and removes a folder labeled RYAN SONG. "Brace yourself, Kai." She hands me a photo.

It's Ryan hanging. He has on a pair of board shorts. No shirt. No shoes. His ten toes appear to dangle over the floor. His face is almost blue and his head turned at an unnatural angle. Beneath him lies a note and a snapshot of Marie. A small table nearby is tipped on its side. The rope around his neck is tied to a chandelier connected to the ceiling by a chain. The photo is stamped: PREFECTURE DE POLICE.

"Sad," I say. But something else is bothering me. Ryan's attire. He looks like any surfer walking down Kalākaua Avenue in Waikīkī. But he's in Paris. In winter. *Board shorts? No shirt or shoes?* I don't say anything about it, just ask, "How did Ryan get on with the other students?"

"Well," she says, "with everyone." She shakes her head. "Here's a copy of the suicide note." It's computer-printed in bold caps: AU REVOIR, MARIE.

"I don't speak French," I admit. "I've never even been to France."

"Au revoir means goodbye," Serena says. "You won't have to know any French. And on the Songs' budget, no way you're going to Paris."

"Okay, then why did Ryan print the note? Why not write it by hand?"

"Printed in bold caps to make a bold statement?" Serena says.

"Seems kind of impersonal," I say. "Where did you get the note?"

"The college requested Ryan's case file from the Paris Police," Serena says. "What was passed on to me is in this folder: The photo, the note, and the police report—translated into English. And here's a DVD about our Paris program and a tourist map." She unfolds on her desk the map displaying major historical sites and buildings.

"So this is Paris?" I gaze at the dizzying maze of streets, each called Rue this or that, and the River Seine that winds through them.

"Our program is hosted by the University of Paris—the Sorbonne—in the Latin Quarter. It's here." She puts her finger on a spot just below the river. "On the Left Bank in the Fifth

Arrondissement—she pronounces it *ah-rhone-dees-mo*—near the Panthéon, that grand domed building."

"I see it." It's in a square called Place du Panthéon.

"Marie moved into Pierre's apartment on that square," Serena says.

"Is she there now?" I ask.

"No, she's traveling around Europe with him," Serena says. "Anyway, we house our students nearby in a glorious old townhouse divided into flats at 44 Rue des Écoles."

"Rue des what?"

"Des Écoles"—she pronounces it *days-eh-coal*—"means, roughly, the street of the schools, because the major centers of learning are there. We rent the third and fourth floors. There is a small lift . . . uh, an elevator . . . that stops only on those two floors. Nobody can ride the lift without an ID card—for the safety and security of our students."

"Only your students had cards?"

"Right. And Russ—Professor Van. And the custodial staff."

"So you had seven students on two floors, which only they had access to?"

"Correct. The floors are also connected by a stairway, but only these two floors. Ryan and Marie both started in single rooms on the third. Until she left, of course."

"Convenient," I say.

Serena shrugs. "Two other students, Kim and Heather, close friends and English majors from Oʻahu, shared a double on the third floor."

"And on the fourth?"

"Three more: Meighan, a French major on scholarship from Michigan, in a single room and Brad and Scooter, business majors and football mates from California, in a double. They weren't stellar students, but did well in Russ's French history course and have since graduated. Actually, all the students did well. I wasn't surprised. We've found studying abroad motivates even less-than-stellar students, and the program tends to draw serious students to begin with. I have Russ's grade records if you'd like to see for yourself."

"Thanks," I say. "And I'd like to talk to the professor too."

"He's beastly busy at present, but I'm sure he'll oblige," she says. "He's applying for the Hilo Hattie Chair. It means more money and less teaching. As you can imagine, the competition is keen."

"I'll wish Professor Van luck," I say, but wonder about a teacher who doesn't want to teach.

"Do me a favor, Kai. When you talk to Russ and the students—and especially to Ryan's parents—tread lightly. We've had enough sadness already."

I repeat her admonition: "Tread lightly."

We talk about Ryan for a few more minutes. Then I walk back to my car in the blazing summer sun.

11

two

From Serena's office I drive through Waikīkī and see some nice sets rolling in. Before long I've got my board in the water and I'm paddling to Pops, or Populars, about a quarter mile offshore from the Sheraton. Pops is cranking—typical of a summer swell. The right-breaking curls seem to sweep from here to eternity. You can tuck into these curls and ride your cares away.

Suicide isn't my favorite kind of case, especially when the deceased is so young. I don't relish the prospect of meeting Ryan's parents later this afternoon. Maybe that's why I've detoured to the surf. Besides, Serena mentioned that Pops was Ryan's favorite spot in town. Can surfing here give me insights into his character? And into the case? I hope so. The facts I've been given so far make me doubt I can tell the Songs much more than they already know.

A wave on the horizon catches my eye. I stroke into position and take it—a nice one about shoulder high. I tuck into the curl and scream along.

Paddling back to the lineup, I think about Ryan. Serena told me he'd been sweet on Marie since high school and apparently hoped their friendship would blossom into romance in Paris. But a few weeks after they arrived for the spring term, Marie met a student at the University of Paris. In what seemed to her friends like a very short time, she and Pierre were living together. Ryan was stung. Far from home and family—Hawai'i was half way around the world—he succumbed to his despair.

The night he died was February 29, Marie's twentieth birthday. She's a leap-year baby. And it turns out she and Pierre had been far from Paris when it happened, celebrating at his parents' home in Lyon. That's the official version of the story, anyway.

I wonder about Ryan killing himself by hanging. No surfer I know of has ever done that. Surfers who die before their time usually get swallowed by a wave or a shark, or by the drugs that have invaded surfing culture. Wave riders go down doing what they love. Or they just go down. A surfer hanging himself would be rare. But Ryan was in Paris when he died and had no waves to chase his blues away. Would a landlocked surfer in despair take his own life?

As many waves as I ride at Pops this morning, none gives me an answer.

three

I shower at Queen's Surf Beach, tote my board back to my car in the Honolulu Zoo lot, put on my street clothes, and head up Kapahulu Avenue to St. Louis Heights. The Songs' home is near the top of the sloping ridge overlooking Waikīkī's skyline. The air up here is cooler. And the sky bluer.

I pull up in front of their island-style bungalow, squeezed between two McMansions that make their place look like servants' quarters. Neat and tidy, but not fancy. In front stands a mango tree that Ryan no doubt climbed as a boy, and a dusty pickup with lettering on the doors that says SONG MASONRY CONTRACTING.

I step across the close-clipped grass to a covered *lānai* and knock on the door. A handsome *hapa* or part-Hawaiian woman greets me. She has the same luminous eyes and shy smile as her son. But her smile cannot mask the sadness in her face.

"Come in," she says, looking too young to be the mother of a twenty-year-old.

The living room continues the neat and tidy theme: rattan couch and chairs and coffee table, a few lamps, and an area rug. Except for a surfboard mounted like a trophy on one wall, which I take to be Ryan's, that's it. And a guitar leaning against another wall. Also his?

"Lono!" she calls into a bedroom. A deeply-tanned local man ambles into the living room. He's wiry—all muscle and bone.

"Sorry about your son." I shake Mr. Song's hand. It's warm but callused hard like concrete.

"My son nevah wen' kill himself," he says in Pidgin. "Nevah!"

"Lono . . . ." His wife tries to calm him.

"My family name been ruin by dis lie!" Mr. Song's face reddens.

"Why don't we sit down," Ryan's mother says, her shy smile fading.

We sit and Mrs. Song says, "Ryan was a serious boy, Mr. Cooke. He didn't always put himself forward, but he was not weak. I know my own boy. I know he would never do this to his father and me."

"Was no coward!" Mr. Song cries. "My son nevah—" He buries his face in his hands.

"I'm sorry, sir," I say again. I'm sure he doesn't hear me.

Mrs. Song keeps her composure. "Ryan was sad when Marie went off with that French boy, but he didn't take it so hard as everyone thinks."

"How do you know?" I ask.

"He sent me emails," she says. "He said, 'I'm okay, Mom. Paris is cool.' He said he was seeing the sights with a girl named Meighan who lived on the next floor."

"Do you still have the emails?"

"Yes. And we have Ryan's laptop. The college mailed it along with his things. Do you want to take it?"

"Sure." I have no idea what use the laptop might be, but with so little to go on I can't afford to pass.

"I'll get it for you before you leave," she says.

"Could Ryan have said he was okay just so you wouldn't worry?" I ask.

"We tell da truth in dis family." Mr. Song uncovers his tear-streamed face. "Jus' prove he nevah do 'em."

"Honey . . . ." His wife puts her hand on his shoulder.

"Are you sure you want me to investigate?" I look into his pained eyes.

They both nod.

"Okay, I'll need a retainer to get started," I say. "Five hundred should do for now." That's half my normal rate.

Mrs. Song disappears and then returns with a rusty Spam can. She pulls out a wad of crumpled bills, flattening them one by one on the coffee table. She counts to five hundred.

I take the bills, but don't feel good about it. Mrs. Song gives me Ryan's laptop, we exchange goodbyes, and I leave.

four

Returning to my Waikīkī Edgewater studio that night I unfold the map of Paris Serena gave me and study the dizzying array of streets and the river that weaves through them. Why Parisians call one bank of the Seine right and the other left doesn't make sense to me. The orientation looks more north and south. But eventually I find the Left Bank and the Latin Quarter. A 5E is printed smack in the middle. That means nothing to me, so I Google it.

> 5ème – Fifth Arrondissement –This neighborhood, the fabled Latin Quarter, takes its name from the Sorbonne, where Latin was the common tongue for all students during the Middle Ages. The neighborhood has the feel of a small village and students mix freely with professionals in its winding streets. Ernest Hemingway and James Joyce lived here, and many other writers, artists, and philosophers . . . .

Not a bad start. Next I locate the domed Panthéon and remember Serena saying Ryan and his fellow students lived nearby on Rue des Écoles. I find it and also the cross street she mentioned as an afterthought: Rue Thénard. I draw a circle around the intersection.

So I have it. The very spot where Ryan Song died.

Hoping to see the actual building, I slip the disk Serena gave me into my DVD player. The program begins with a brassy version of the French national anthem—same as the horn opening to the Beatles' "All You Need is Love." The major monuments and tourist attractions of Paris flash by on the screen. And in case I might miss any of them, a sonorous voiceover identifies each. Then the pitch begins:

> *Paradise College, International Studies Division, welcomes you to Paris. Imagine living and studying in this world-famous city most people only dream of visiting. Paris, the city of lights. Paris, the city of love. That's you atop the Eiffel Tower! That's you admiring the Mona Lisa at the Louvre. That's you in a sidewalk café watching the glamour of Parisian life stroll by. It's a once-in-a-lifetime opportunity, and it can be yours!*

Sign me up—I'm sold already. Soon the narrator gets to student accommodations.

> *You will live in an historic nineteenth-century town home, apportioned into single and double rooms expressly for Paradise College students, at the illustrious address: 44 Rue des Écoles . . . .*

I freeze the image. It's an elegant building—six stories, by my count—with a Mansard roof, clay chimneys, tall windows, wrought iron balconies, and blooming planters. On the ground floor is a florist called *L'ile aux Fleurs* that reminds me of the *lei* shop beneath my office. Only more chic.

I press PLAY and the video continues with course options, excursions, and the school calendar, concluding with another round of Paris images. I keep waiting for the price tag. But it never comes. The sonorous voice merely says, "A semester in Paris is more affordable than you might imagine . . . ." And that's it.

I eject the DVD and turn to the police report. Paris Police have a more elegant way of saying a young man hung himself than Honolulu Police do. The English translation, sprinkled with French phrases, says the American student took his own life as a result of feelings of dejection and despair over his spurned love for a beautiful young woman. And he did so fittingly and symbolically on the evening of her birthday. The suicide note—AU REVOIR, MARIE—and her photo are evidence *irréfutable*. A summary of statements by Ryan's professor and fellow students corroborate this. The fact that Ryan apparently took the rope *impulsivement* from a maintenance room in the building further suggests his desperation. He was pronounced dead at the scene at four minutes after nine on Wednesday morning, March first. It's estimated that death occurred the night before, no later than ten o'clock. Considering the absence of other motives, and after interviews with persons who might shed light on the incident *regrettable*, the case was closed.

five

The next morning I drive to the Kakaʻako campus of Paradise College to interview Professor Russell Van, whose cramped office smells of pipe tobacco and musty books. He extends a cool pink palm with the grip of a gummy bear, so unlike the warm firm hand of Ryan's father. The professor points to a chair and I sit.

"You're here about Ryan?" he says with a hint of nervousness in his voice. His double chin and aloha shirt blousing around his waist reveal an indolence I thought no longer in fashion in the academy. But Professor Van is obviously an old-timer.

I nod. "I read the summary of your statement to the Paris Police and hoped you wouldn't mind telling me what happened in your own words."

"So his parents don't think he did it?" the professor says. "Let me tell you, I saw him hanging there over the snapshot of her. How can there be any doubt?"

"Did you talk with him before it happened?"

"When Marie moved in with that French student, it bothered Ryan. He just wasn't himself. I emailed Serena and she said to call him in."

"Did you?"

"I did. Ryan said little. Just that he'd be okay. He really didn't want to talk about it."

"Did you talk with him again?"

"No——" Van hesitates. "Well, he did come to see me a few days later. But not about Marie. About something else."

"What?"

"It was unrelated. So I didn't even mention it to the police." Van rocks back uneasily in his chair. "He said he wanted to discuss the next exam."

"Was he worried about his grade?"

"I doubt it. He was carrying an A-minus. Anyway, I'll never know. I was on my way to a lecture on the medieval French *ballade* when he came in. I told Ryan I'd be back in an hour, but he didn't return. The next time I saw him was on that awful morning."

"Would you mind telling me what you saw?"

"When I got there all the students—except Marie, of course—were standing outside Ryan's door. He was hanging very still."

"How did the students react?"

"Meighan was crying. But the others just looked dumbstruck."

"Is that what you expected?"

"When you take these island kids to a place like Paris, you don't know what to expect." He arches his woolly brows. "For many, it's their first time away from Hawai'i. Some handle it, others don't."

"Did they handle it?"

"For the most part, except for Ryan. All seven took my French history course, which included excursions to the Bastille, Versailles, etc. So I got to know them fairly well. I usually teach the course as a large lecture with standardized exams. But this was a small, intimate group. To keep the course on par I used the same exams, but otherwise I ran it like a seminar."

"Did Ryan spend time with anybody besides Marie?"

"Sometimes with Meighan. Sometimes with Kim and Heather."

"What about Brad and Scooter?"

"I was told the guys went to the *Folies Bergère* together. But Brad and Scooter's appetite—and budget—for cabarets apparently exceeded Ryan's. Not to mention Brad's appetite for the dancers."

"The two guys partied *and* got good grades?"

"When you're twenty you can do things we older folks can't." Van rocks forward in his chair.

"And Marie—what was she like?"

"One of my best students ever. An A-plus. I rarely give those."

"I never saw one," I say. "But if I care to see hers, Serena said I can look at your grade records."

"Don't bother. They won't tell you anything about Ryan you don't already know." The professor frowns. "I'll never teach in Paris again. What happened there ruined it for me. I haven't slept well since, even with the little pills my doctor gave me. Best to stay here and finish my book, anyway."

"To help your chances for the Hilo Hattie Chair?"

Van looks surprised. "How did you know?"

"Serena told me." I stand and thank him. "Good luck winning that Chair, sir."

He lets out a breath as I leave his office, seeming relieved the interview is over. Why? Whatever could make the professor anxious if he's so sure Ryan took his own life?

six

From Paradise College I stop by the Waikīkī Edgewater and send identical emails to the five students I plan to interview on Oʻahu. I send a different email to Marie, who Serena said is traveling in Europe. The email to Marie contains questions; the emails to the others contain a request to meet.

Moments later a reply arrives from meighan616@ pc.edu: "I'm still very sad about Ryan but will try to talk with you. Call me. Meighan McMannis."

She was first to find Ryan hanging, according to Serena, so it seems appropriate to interview her first.

I call Meighan and arrange to meet her at a Starbucks near Ward Centre. She says she's taking a summer course in French and will stop by after class.

I'm sipping a decaf when the green-eyed Michigan blonde steps in toting her French textbook. She's no frail flower but a solid, sturdy young woman who looks as if she could endure those frigid Midwestern winters. She orders a large latte and joins me. The animated conversations going on around us assure me we won't be overheard.

"Ryan was a sweet guy." Meighan fixes her green eyes on me and sips her latte. "I loved him."

I say nothing. Just wait.

"I mean, it's not like that." She seems surprised at what she's said. "He was just a good, gentle soul."

"You said in your statement that you were the first to find Ryan. Can you tell me how that happened?"

"Sure. Heather called and asked me to check on Ryan. She hadn't seen him and was worried. So I went down to his room. The door was unlocked."

"You lived on the fourth floor, right? And Heather and Kim lived on the third, same as Ryan?"

She nods.

"Why didn't Heather check on him herself?"

"I don't know. She just asked if I'd mind and I didn't. So I went."

"What time?"

"About eight on Wednesday morning. I knocked on his door. There was no answer. I knocked again and then tried the knob. The door opened. I saw him."

"Did you go into the room?"

"Not really." She grips her coffee. Her hands tremble. "It was kind of . . . uh, a shock. And I didn't want to disturb anything."

"So you did or didn't go into his room?"

"I didn't." Her eyes glisten. "Look, I'm only trying to help Ryan's mom and dad. But I feel like you're interrogating me."

"Sorry," I say, then press on. "What did you do after you saw Ryan?"

"I banged on Heather and Kim's door. I was crying. They knew right away something was wrong. All three of us walked back to Ryan's room and I opened the door again."

"How did Heather and Kim react?"

"Heather gasped and said, 'Oh, my God!' or something like that. Kim asked, 'What should we do?'"

"I said we should call the police. Heather said we should call Professor Van first. And that's what we did."

"Why call the professor before the police?"

"I don't know. It wasn't my idea. But Heather insisted."

"Where were Brad and Scooter when all this was happening?"

"I'm coming to that. They sometimes partied all night and then slept in the next day. We didn't know if we should wake them. But Heather said—'Let's get 'em.' So she and I walked upstairs and knocked on their door. I was surprised when it opened right away."

"They weren't hung over—sleeping it off?"

"Brad looked better than Scooter, who'd obviously been drinking. But Brad said they both had a test that morning and had stayed up studying. We took them down to Ryan's room."

"And how did Brad and Scooter react?"

"Brad covered his face. Scooter just stared with a kind of wonder in his eyes. Then Professor Van showed up and walked into Ryan's room, looked around, and called the police. When they came we had to leave the building and wait down on the sidewalk. An officer who spoke English interviewed each of us separately. By the time they let us back upstairs, Ryan had been taken away."

"And you didn't go back into his room after that?"

"No, not after they took him away."

Meighan has contradicted herself.   First she said she didn't go into Ryan's room, and then she implied she did. Either she's confused or withholding information.

"Hey, thanks," I say and finish my decaf. "Can I give you a ride back to campus?"

"Nah, I'll just stay here and study my French."

I stand and say the only French I know. *"Au revoir."*

She sits bolt upright.

"What's wrong?"

"The note," she says. "Ryan's suicide note."

seven

I drive to my office on the corner of Maunakea and Beretania Streets in Chinatown. I'm on the second floor above Fujiyama's Flower Leis. The jasmine scent of pikake *lei* being strung inside the shop follows me up the stairs—assuaging in some way the sad business I've gotten myself into. Unlocking my door, I glance at the longboard rider airbrushed there and SURFING DETECTIVE: CONFIDENTIAL INVESTIGATIONS—ALL ISLANDS and wonder again why I'm investigating a suicide in Paris. Ryan was a surfer. That's the best I can do.

I check my emails: I have new ones from Heather and Scooter. Heather says I can meet her and her friend Kimberly at Magic Island this afternoon. Scooter says he can see me at the Outback Steakhouse in Hawai'i Kai tomorrow. I confirm both interviews, then head to Magic Island.

Heather and Kimberly are sitting on a bench by the seawater lagoon when I pull up. Magic Island is not really an island, but a grassy peninsula on the Diamond Head end of Ala Moana Beach Park with the lagoon at the point. Beyond that is a sea wall and crashing surf.

The two twenty-something island girls are in running gear—tank tops, shorts, and trainers. Heather has long black hair, soft curves, and a fuller, more luxuriant figure than her friend's. Kimberly, by contrast, is lean and pony-tailed. They tell me they both work at a boutique at Ala Moana Shopping Center, not far from their apartment on Pi'ikoi Street.

After a few pleasantries I ask Heather, "Why did you ask Meighan to look in on Ryan? Why not just walk across the hall yourselves?"

There's silence for a moment. Kim swings her ponytail around and gives Heather a look that says, *Say something!*

"I did," Heather leans toward me, her gaping top revealing more of her than a PI working a case ought to see. *A distraction?* "Kim and I both did," she says. "But Ryan didn't answer. So we went back to our room and called Meighan."

"Why not just open Ryan's door? Hadn't you done that before?"

"Yeah, but this time it didn't feel right." Heather again. "We thought Ryan was with someone."

"Who? Not Marie. She was miles away."

Kim finally chimes in. "Meighan."

"Meighan?" I must sound surprised. Kim covers her mouth.

Heather gives her a look and then to me says, "It's no secret Meighan liked Ryan. When Marie left, Meighan kind of . . . well, made her move."

As my interview with the two friends progresses, I compare what they say with their statements in the police report, and also with the version of events already supplied by Professor Van and Meighan. It quickly becomes clear that Kim is the sidekick and Heather calls the shots. All the time the latter is talking, something's bugging me. I got the same feeling listening to Meighan and the professor. While their statements are all uncannily consistent, something is being left out. What?

I ask several more questions, with the same results. Finally, I say, "You can speak freely to me. I'm not the police. I'm just trying to help out Ryan's mom and dad. And I'm not suggesting either of you did anything wrong."

Kim looks pale. Heather pipes up, "We *are* speaking freely. We've told you everything."

"And I'm very grateful," I reply. "If you happen to think of anything else, would you please call or email?" I hand them both my card.

They nod.

I stand and turn toward my car, then turn back again and say, "Oh, one more thing. Do either of you know any reason why someone might want to harm Ryan?"

The two friends look startled. Predictably it's Heather who speaks. "Why would you ask such a question?"

"Sorry. I have to."

"Then all I can say," Heather responds, "is not really. Ryan was a super nice guy."

"So I've heard."

I walk back to my car wondering what these Paradise College students and their professor aren't telling me.

eight

The next day I get an email from Marie. She says she's in Stuttgart, Germany, and heading for Heidelberg.

Dear Kai,

It's so sad about Ryan. I really miss him.

Yes, the police report was correct. I was away from Paris when Ryan died. An officer interviewed me after I returned. I'm afraid I wasn't very helpful because I hadn't really talked much with Ryan since early February.

I sent him an email then, trying to explain about Pierre. I told Ryan he would always be a dear friend. And that I hoped he would understand. We didn't talk much after that.

I still feel terrible about what happened. He was such a sweet guy. Everybody liked him. I can't think of anyone who didn't.

Please send my condolences again to Ryan's parents and let me know if you have more questions.

Aloha, Marie

I don't see the need, at this point, to question Marie further. A girl who's broken a guy's heart has little reason to wish him further harm. If she has a conscience, as Marie apparently has, she feels bad enough already. So unless Marie is an accomplished liar and unless the others are covering for her, there isn't much reason to suspect her of anything other than the bad timing of Ryan turning up dead on her birthday.

nine

That afternoon I drive to the Outback Steakhouse in Hawai'i Kai to interview Scooter. The restaurant is perched on Kalaniana'ole Highway across from Maunalua Bay and flanked by the twin volcanic mounds of Koko Head and Koko Crater. Walking to the restaurant from my car I watch a windsurfer etch a frothy white trail across the bay and remember that I haven't heard from Scooter's buddy, Brad. I'll ask about that.

A big guy with curls framing his baby-boy face smiles when I ask for Scooter. I should have looked at his nametag. He has fifty pounds on me, easy. I recall Serena saying Scooter and his pal Brad played high school football together. We sit in the empty waiting room during the lull between lunch and dinner.

Scooter removes his server apron with meaty paws and says, "Too bad about Ryan." His voice is soft for such a large man. And he sounds almost sincere.

"Too bad," I say.

He then gives me a version of the same story I've heard before. It's consistent with his earlier statement, but like the other students he sounds rehearsed. Somewhere near the end of his spiel he says he didn't go into Ryan's room on the night he died.

"But you did go into Ryan's room at other times?" I ask.

"Yeah, hanging out. We hung out in each other's rooms."

Hanging? Hung? Scooter seems oblivious to his inappropriate choice of words. But I say nothing.

"Professor Van said you and Brad hit some clubs with Ryan, but you didn't do much with him after that. How come?"

"We were into different stuff—that's all."

"I'm curious, Scooter." I shift gears. "Why does a business major with no background in French go to Paris and study French history?"

"I dunno." He looks bewildered. "A buddy of ours took Professor Van's course and liked it, so Brad and I decided— why not go to Paris?"

"Just like that?"

"Yeah . . . well, we had to apply and get financial aid, but—"

"You didn't have trouble with the language?"

"Not really. They spoke English in the courses we took."

"Serena said you did well in Professor Van's course."

"Uh . . . 'cause I liked it, I guess."

"No doubt," I say. "Say, do you know how I can get in touch with Brad? He hasn't answered my email."

"Yeah. He's working in Waikīkī at the Moana Surfrider— front desk." Scooter rattles off Brad's number.

Finally I ask if Scooter knows of anyone who might want to hurt Ryan, and get the same response I got from the others—a startled look and the professed disbelief that such a fine person could be intentionally harmed by another.

Leaving the restaurant, I turn back and see Scooter pulling out his cell phone. He's calling Brad to tip him off that I'm coming. So I wait.

When I get back to my car, I try Brad. He doesn't sound surprised to hear from me. And he doesn't sound enthusiastic when he agrees to meet with me at the Surfrider.

ten

I park at the foot of Diamond Head and walk down oceanfront Kalākaua Avenue into Waikīkī. The Surfrider is the first hotel on the beach. A balmy breeze wafts through the open-air lobby. Beyond it, tourists glisten on the white sand and bob in the turquoise sea. Two clerks are working the desk—a redheaded girl and a tall guy with ice-blue eyes. Brad has the looks of a TV anchorman and the physique of an NFL linebacker. Even in his hotel uniform he looks powerful.

We shake hands and Brad says, "I can talk until we get traffic at the desk." He turns to the redhead. "Uh, this is Amber."

Amber says, "Hi."

So we get the formalities out of the way and move beyond her earshot.

"Really too bad about Ryan," Brad says, sounding like his buddy.

"Too bad," I say again. It's becoming my automatic response.

"His death hit us all hard," Brad continues, "and kind of pulled us together."

"How's that?"

Just then a twenty-something in a dripping bikini glides up to the desk. His eyes lock on her. I remember Van's commenting on Brad's appetite for cabaret dancers. But the bikini goes to Amber. A shadow crosses his face.

"Look, I shouldn't tell you," he bends toward me and lowers his voice, "but you'll probably find out anyway."

"Tell me what?" I ask.

"About Heather and me. We started up a kind of thing in Paris."

"And?"

"Well . . . man, she's pregnant!"

I try to keep a straight face. Then I remember the extra flesh Heather is carrying. *Could be.*

"Her roommate doesn't even know," he says. "It wasn't exactly planned."

"Why are you telling me this?" I'm curious. "Does it have anything to do with Ryan?"

"No, but you're a detective. You'd find out about Heather and me anyway. I'm telling you the truth about us so you'll know I'm telling the truth about Ryan."

"Okay, so tell me."

Then he starts in on the same story Scooter and the others told. And, like them, he sounds canned. He sticks almost precisely to his statement in the police report. Often people alter something, if ever so slightly, in the retelling. But Brad's reprise is dead on. I just let him talk. The more he thinks I believe him, the better my chances to gain his cooperation later, if necessary.

When I ask if he knows anyone who might want to hurt Ryan, Brad says the only person he can think of is Marie.

"I meant bodily harm," I say. "Do you think Marie capable of that?"

Brad shrugs. "She's got her dark side. And she sure could have cared more about Ryan's feelings."

"I suppose."

I ask Brad a few more questions, then walk back to my car, sorting out what he said. Why did he tell me Heather is pregnant? And why did he point suspicion at Marie? Brad seems smart enough not to simply blurt these things out—unless he has a reason.

eleven

I drive to Starbucks, order a coffee, and wait. It's about the same time I interviewed Meighan yesterday. If she's a creature of habit, like most people, she'll show up before long.

No sooner do I sit down with my coffee than the Michigan blonde pushes open the door, walks to the counter, and orders a latte. When it's ready she turns to look for a table. I stand and wave.

"What a surprise," I say. "Do you come here often?"

"Funny," Meighan says, "I didn't think you were the Starbucks type."

"I'm not," I say.

She gives me a look.

"As long as you're here, what do you say we talk a bit more about Ryan? You know, just to clear up loose ends."

"Fine." She glances down at her frothy latte.

"You said Heather asked you to check on Ryan. Right?"

"That's right." She sips her coffee.

"Then you went down to his room, the door was open, and you walked in."

She nods and takes another sip.

"Then what?"

"I saw Ryan hanging and then I ran and got Heather and Kim."

"But what did you do *inside* his room?"

"I didn't go in."

"But you just said you did."

She turns away. "I don't want to talk about it."

"Look, Meighan, if Paradise College finds out you withheld information about Ryan's death, you don't want to know the consequences." It's an empty threat, but the best I can come up with.

She sits in silence, sipping her latte and apparently weighing what I said. I have no idea which way she'll go. The defiance in her eyes suggests I've lost the battle. But suddenly her look softens and she says, "Okay, I did find Ryan hanging in his room, but not like everybody thinks. He was naked."

"Naked—as in nude?"

She nods.

"No board shorts?" My instincts about his attire were apparently right.

"He had nothing on." Meighan grips her cup. "I didn't want him to be found that way, so I slipped on the shorts."

"You weren't embarrassed seeing him naked, or squeamish touching his skin?"

"Well, no." She blushes. "I'd, uh, seen him before."

"You had?" If Meighan was intimate with Ryan after Marie left, maybe he wasn't as brokenhearted as everybody but his own mother is saying.

"I'd rather not go into it." Meighan looks away.

"Okay. Then what happened?"

She faces me again. "I left the room. And when I came back with the others, I didn't say anything about the board shorts."

"Did Heather or Kim say anything beyond what you already told me?"

"Not much. Well, Kim whispered to Heather. And then Heather put her finger to her lips."

"And what did you make of that?" I know the answer but I want to hear it from her.

"That they already knew Ryan had hung himself?"

I leave my coffee on the table on my way out.

twelve

A crack has opened in the wall of deceit. Concerned that Meighan might talk to Heather and Kim, I drive immediately to their apartment. I park in view of their second-floor flat at the Piʻikoi Arms, a faded, low-rise slab building near Ala Moana Shopping Center. I call their number. No answer. It's around the time they come home from their jobs. I trust my stake-out won't last long.

I'm wrong. I wait a half hour. Then another. I'm about to pack it in when Heather strolls by and climbs the stairs. I let her go. I don't want her—I want her sidekick. I wait. Kim eventually walks by and I pop out of my car.

"What are you doing here?" She looks curious, even cracks a smile.

"I was in the neighborhood and was worried about you."

"Worried about me? Why?"

"Because you don't deserve to go down for Ryan's death. I doubt you had anything to do with it. But you're putting yourself at risk by sticking with your friends who did."

"What do you mean? Ryan committed suicide."

"Take a deep breath, Kim, and please listen to reason."

"Okay."

"You and Heather knew Ryan was dead that morning before you asked Meighan to check on him."

Her smile fades. "It wasn't my idea."

"I know, but why pretend to have Meighan find him?"

"Heather knocked and Ryan didn't answer," Kimberly explains. "But we figured he was there because I'd heard noise in his room at about nine the night before."

"What kind of noise?"

"Like furniture moving."

"Heather didn't hear it?"

"She wasn't there. Heather had a stomach ache that night and went to the pharmacy."

It wasn't a stomach ache, I think. But Kim doesn't need to know her roommate is pregnant until Heather is ready to tell her.

"So what really happened the next morning?" I ask.

"When Ryan didn't answer we opened the door and saw him hanging. And I guess we just got scared."

"Scared of what?"

"Of finding him like that."

"C'mon, Kim, I'm trying to keep you out of trouble—but you have to cooperate and tell me the truth."

"Believe me," she says, "I had nothing to do with it. I liked Ryan. I would never dream of hurting him."

"I know you wouldn't hurt Ryan. But somebody did. I need to know who and why."

"I told you, I don't know."

"I think you do. You can tell me or you can tell HPD."

Another empty threat, but she thinks it over.

"Kim?" I coax her. "What's it going to be?"

She hesitates, then finally opens her mouth and the words tumble out: "I think Ryan's death might have had something to do with cheating."

"Cheating on who?"

"Not cheating on a person. Cheating on exams."

"Whose exams?"

"Professor Van's."

"Ryan cheated? That doesn't sound like him."

"Not Ryan. He caught someone with the answers to all the exams. I don't want to say who." She hesitates. "Ryan didn't think it was fair for this person to party while the rest of us worked."

Most college students party. The seven who went to Paris would be no exception. But only two of them are reputed party animals. It's most likely one or the other, or both. I don't press Kim. I don't need to. But I ask, "Why do you think Ryan's death had to do with this cheating?"

"He told the person to stop or he'd go to Professor Van."

"Did the person stop?"

"No."

"Then why didn't Ryan go to the professor?" I recall that Van had said nothing to me about cheating.

"Ryan *did* go to Professor Van."

"He did?" Was Van involved too?

"Yeah, Ryan told me the Prof. would speak to us about it."

"Did Professor Van speak to you?"

"Not to me or Heather."

"Did he speak to anyone? Did he do anything?"

She shrugs. "I don't know."

Before I can respond she cries, "Shit! Heather's going to kill me!" and runs into the Pi'ikoi Arms.

thirteen

First thing the next morning I take up Serena on her offer to see the professor's grade computations. I can't help wondering about Van. Why did he do nothing to stop the alleged cheating? Why did he withhold information from the college and the Paris Police? And from me?

I pick up a large brown envelope from Serena's assistant and open it as I step back into the morning sun. Inside is a single sheet with the names of the seven students and columns displaying exam scores, semester averages, and letter grades. What immediately strikes me as odd is that all seven—except Ryan, of course—finished the term with an A. There are a few minuses and one plus—for Marie, as Van told me—but no grade less than A. Not one B. Not one C. How often does that happen in an undergraduate course?

I check the students' individual exam scores and find, not to my surprise, that both Brad and Scooter—the business major party animals—had the highest marks in French History next to Marie's. From one exam to the next, a few points separate the two. But their scores, otherwise, follow a nearly identical pattern. Then I remember two things:

Van telling me he used the same exams in Paris as he had in Hawai'i, and Scooter telling me a friend had taken Van's course in a previous term. *Bingo*: Scooter got the exams from his friend and brought them to Paris.

Then I notice something else curious. Heather's and Kim's scores begin in the 70s, but about mid-way through the term, when Ryan died, their scores rise nearly twenty points into the 90s. Did they suddenly start studying? When I check their grades for the later part of the term against Brad and Scooter's, I find the same pattern. Mulling it over, Heather's and Kim's dramatic improvement makes sense. If Heather and Brad were lovers, he would naturally share the exams with her. And Heather would share them with her friend Kim.

But what I'm not prepared for are Meighan's scores. Hers start higher than those of either Heather or Kim—fitting for a scholarship student—then shoot up even further about mid-term, following the same pattern. *Were they* all *cheating?*

Not the best and brightest of the bunch. Not Ryan's unrequited love, Marie. Her A-plus clearly distinguishes her from the others. But just to be thorough I check her record. Marie's scores begin exceptionally high. On the first exam she hits 98 percent. On the second, a perfect 100. She stands head and shoulders above the pack. When I scan her scores to mid-term, my jaw drops and I recall Brad saying Marie had a dark side. Her marks continue high—but take on the same pattern as Brad's, Scooter's, and the others. Did she quit studying and start coasting? Why would a brilliant student cheat when she could earn an A-plus on her own?

Ryan knew the answer. But he's no longer alive to tell.

fourteen

Later that afternoon I paddle back out to Pops—Ryan's favorite break. The waves are rolling in three to four feet. Traffic is light. It's a weekday and the regulars aren't off work yet. I get a couple of rides. Then I wait between sets—and try to put together the pieces I've gathered on the case.

Kim told the truth about the cheating. But she failed to mention that not just one person was cheating—the entire class was cheating. Herself included. If Professor Van couldn't see it, he was blind. Or had he turned a blind eye?

All seven students lied. Their professor, at minimum, withheld information and abdicated his responsibilities to them and to the college. Are they still covering for each other—all of them involved in Ryan's death?

fifteen

Back in my Waikīkī apartment that night I check the mail program on Ryan's laptop. Oddly, I find no personal messages from early February before he died, only generic and junk emails. What puzzles me more is that I find not even the emails between Ryan and his mother that she mentioned. These personal messages might reveal Ryan's state of mind— and also contributing factors to his death. In other words, they're essential.

Then I realize that since Ryan had been a long way from home—in Paris, not in Honolulu—he would have used webmail rather than his laptop's mail program, connected no doubt to a Honolulu server. With a little searching I find his webmail link. The inbox looks identical to the other. No personal emails. All have apparently been deleted. Then I remember that deleting messages from webmail doesn't necessarily remove them. Deleted emails go to a trash folder where they remain—unless or until they are expunged.

I open the trash folder. *Bingo!* The missing emails have been deleted but, fortunately, not expunged. I'm surprised the Paris Police overlooked this.

The first is an email sent by Ryan to his mother after Marie moved from Rue des Écoles—the email Mrs. Song told me about.

> I'm okay, Mom. Paris is cool. I'm seeing
> the sights with a girl named Meighan . . .

I have to agree with Mrs. Song that he doesn't sound too shook up about Marie. I scan further until I find one sent to Scooter dated February 24th—five days before Ryan died.

> Scooter, I know you and Brad have the
> answers to Professor Van's exams. That's
> not fair to the rest of us. Do the right thing,
> brah.

"Not fair to the rest of us," suggests that at this point only Scooter and Brad had the exams, which is corroborated by Van's grade sheet. I check Ryan's inbox for an answer from Scooter. None. But I find one from Brad dated February 26th.

> If you know what's good for you, Ryan,
> you'll mind your own fucking business.

I look for more emails between Ryan and the two guys, but find none. If the battle of words escalated, it must have been through verbal exchanges rather than emails.

Next I check Ryan's laptop for documents. If the suicide note was printed from his computer, the document still might be there. But I can't find it, of course. Until I click the trash icon on his desktop. There it is: AU REVOIR, MARIE

The document was created on March 1 at 2:13 am, Paris time (to which the laptop is still set). That's several hours after Ryan reportedly died. He couldn't have printed the note himself. And whoever trashed it afterward neglected to empty the trash.

No wonder the Paris Police failed to mention these documents in their report. They may have given Ryan's laptop a cursory look, and found nothing.

The emails and the faked suicide note provide evidence that Ryan was murdered because he threatened to expose cheating in Van's history class. That the cheating became more widespread, involving every student except Ryan, means all had a motive to cover up. What I need is specifics—who did what and when. What I need is somebody to talk. I don't expect Brad or Scooter will implicate themselves. And I don't expect Heather will let Kim talk to me again. With Marie accessible only by email, that leaves Meighan.

Serena gave me her address: the Marco Polo, a once swanky seventies-era condo on Kapiolani Boulevard overlooking the Ala Wai Canal and Waikīkī. I drive there hoping to find her at home.

It's late. You can't get into the Marco Polo at night without a pass card, so I follow a resident in. Meighan lives on the 27th floor in a studio apartment facing the mountains, rather than the water. I knock. The Michigan blonde opens and doesn't look surprised to see me.

"Meighan, I know now Ryan was murdered," I say. "I'm here to give you one last chance to clear yourself. Some of your classmates already have."

She doesn't even blink. "Come inside."

Meighan leads me into her tiny studio apartment. We sit on the edge of her bed, which also serves as a couch.

"Tell me everything," I say. "And don't leave anything out this time."

"Okay. I was telling you the truth when I said I found Ryan hanging in his room naked. I couldn't believe he'd do that."

"He didn't."

"I know he didn't, but I didn't know it then."

"When did you find out?"

"Later that morning. When Heather, Kim and I got Brad and Scooter, they all acted shocked, like I told you, but I could tell they were faking. They were saying phony stuff like, 'Oh, it's so sad.' None of it seemed real."

"What happened next?"

"I finally said 'I don't believe this. Ryan wouldn't hang himself.' Then Brad snarled, 'You better shut your face. You're involved as much as we are.' Brad could get violent when he was angry. I'd already seen that."

"What did you see?"

"About a week before, Heather came to class one day with a black eye. She said she fell on the stairs. We all knew she was sleeping with Brad and we all figured he just went off on her, for whatever reason."

"She didn't confide in you or Kim about it?"

"Not me. Maybe Kim," Meighan says. "But Heather usually defended Brad—made excuses for him. You know how it goes."

"Unfortunately," I say. "The cycle of domestic abuse."

"Anyway, that's why I was scared of him," Meighan confesses. "That's why I went along when he said we all had to stick together. He said if Ryan's death looked suspicious, the cheating might come out."

"Did you already have the exam answers when Ryan died?"

She bows her head and lowers her voice. *"Yes.* They gave them to me a few days before. But I didn't use them—"

"Until afterward." I complete her sentence.

She nods slowly. Her eyes moisten.

"Why did you cheat? Aren't you on scholarship?"

"That's just it. I've got to maintain an A-minus average to keep my scholarship. I wanted to have fun in Paris and I thought—*stupidly*—that the answers would give me a little more time. I had no idea any harm would come to Ryan. Honest!"

"How did harm come to him?"

"When he found out Scooter and Brad had the exam answers and wouldn't stop cheating, Ryan told the rest of us. Then Heather went straight to Brad."

"Brad wasn't sharing the exams with her already?"

"I don't think so," Meighan says. "But he gave them to her then. And to Kim and to everyone else."

"To Ryan?"

"He tried, but Ryan wouldn't take them."

"Who hanged him?"

"I never asked. It was too horrible. And too stupid. Ryan was hanging there naked. So unlike him. That's why I slipped the board shorts on him—before I knew what really happened. Later Heather put the photo of Marie under him. And Kim typed the suicide note on Ryan's laptop. She didn't know much French, but she did know *au revoir.*"

"Was Marie involved?"

"No. I guess she still thinks Ryan hanged himself and she still feels guilty. Like it was her fault—because she moved in with Pierre."

"Then why did Marie cheat?"

Meighan looks surprised. "How'd you find out?"

"We detectives have our ways," I say. "Anyhow, wasn't Marie a brilliant student?"

"Yes, but when she moved in with Pierre she sort of flipped. Suddenly she's living in Paris with a French guy. All she wanted was to spend time with him. She's no angel, but I can't blame her. Being with Pierre was more important to her than anything."

sixteen

The next day I call Professor Van and tell him I know Ryan Song had complained to him about cheating in his history course. And I know that Van concealed this information from the Paris Police, from Paradise College, and from me. I ask him why.

"Are you going public with this?" he asks.

"Depends," I say.

"Ryan is dead," he replies. "That can't be changed."

"But you might have saved his life. I guess you were more concerned about your reputation—about how it might look if so many of your students got caught cheating."

"Ryan brought me accusations, not proof."

"I saw your grade records, Professor," I say.

Van is quiet.

"A scandal like this," I say, "and you can kiss the Hilo Hattie Chair goodbye."

"Are you going public?" he asks again.

seventeen

I call Scooter's cell phone after talking to Van and ask if I can see him one last time to wrap up my investigation. I can barely hear him over the blare of hip-hop music, but he says "Didn't find anything, eh?"

"How'd you guess?" I reply.

"Too bad, man!" He sounds pleased, rather than sorry. "I'm at the Z Lounge. Brad's with me."

"Hang on," I say. "I'll be there in fifteen."

"Uh, we'll hang on. We're not going anywhere."

I hop in my car and am there in less than ten. The Z Lounge is a hostess bar and strip joint on a seedy block of Kona Street. The odor of stale beer and cigarettes hits me as I step into the darkness. Hip-hop blares. You can't smoke in here anymore, but before the law was changed the dark paneled walls got saturated. The proprietor, a former madam named Michi, knows how to keep customers coming with exotic dancers and happy hour specials. It's too early for either, so there aren't any customers except Brad and Scooter who sit alone at the bar with their beers. Take that back—a young woman from the establishment has her arm around Brad and a drink in front of her.

I take the stool next to Scooter and order a beer. He turns to me.

"So you're wrapping up, huh?" he asks.

"You bet," I reply.

"Don't tell Heather." Brad gestures to the woman with her arm around him and winks.

"My lips are sealed," I say.

"We feel really sorry for Ryan's parents," Brad continues, "but they should have saved their money. Oh well, at least you got a gig."

"That I did," I say.

"So what's left to wrap up?" Scooter asks.

"Oh, I just wondered who put the rope around his neck." I sip my beer. "Was it you or Brad?"

"Huh?" Scooter clinks his bottle on the bar. "What are you talking about?"

"Ryan," I say, "which one of you handled the rope?"

"Hey, man," Brad says in a menacing tone, "can't you see there's a lady present?" She smiles. "Anyway," he continues, "Ryan committed suicide."

"He didn't," I say.

"He didn't?" Scooter puts on a dumb look.

"You guys had it all planned. But what you didn't plan on was somebody talking. Or somebody checking Ryan's laptop."

"This is bullshit, man!" Brad fumes. "What do you think you're doing, coming in here and saying this kind of crap to us? Do you think you're funny? Or are you just a complete asshole?"

"Point is, Brad, you and Scooter hung Ryan because he found out you had answers to Professor Van's exams. First you tried to shut him up by threatening him and then by giving him the answers. But that didn't work because Ryan wouldn't take them. He refused to cheat. That pissed you off even more. And it put you in jeopardy—because if Ryan told Van, you two would flunk the course and not graduate. So then you cooked up a scheme to make Ryan's murder look like a suicide. You coerced Kim and Heather and Meighan into helping and kept them quiet by threatening to implicate them if they talked. It was a halfway decent plan. And it worked—for a while."

Brad and Scooter glance at each other. I put a five on the bar, stand, and turn toward the door.

"So what happens now?" Scooter looks bewildered.

"Did you guys like France?" I ask.

"Yeah," he replies. "It was cool. Why?"

"Because that's where you'll probably do your time."

I step from the reek and darkness into the afternoon sun.

eighteen

When I cross Kona Street and walk to my car, I hear my name called from behind. It's Scooter, pushing open the door of the Z Lounge and following me. He jogs across the street and comes toward me. Instinctively I pop open the trunk to my Smith & Wesson—in case Scooter gets nasty.

"Kai, wait." Scooter stops a few feet from me. He doesn't look angry. Just kind of confused. "You've got it wrong."

"Got what wrong?" I stand by my open trunk, eyeing the revolver. "You guys are going down for what you did. No question."

"I didn't do it," he says. "It wasn't me in Ryan's room with Brad. It was Heather. *She* put the rope around his neck."

"Who are you trying to kid?" I say, dumbfounded at his stupidity. "Heather was at the pharmacy, complaining of a sore tummy. But actually she's pregnant, if you don't already know."

"I know she's pregnant. But she wasn't at the pharmacy when Ryan died—like she told Kim and everyone else. The pharmacy on Rue des Écoles closes at eight. She was in Ryan's room with Brad. She asked Brad to go with her because she was freaked out about getting caught cheating. They didn't intend to hurt Ryan. Just to talk. But Brad got pissed off, like he always does, and knocked Ryan down. He hit the floor really hard and went limp. They didn't wait to find out if he was passed out or dead. The got a rope from the utility closet, stripped off his clothes, and strung him up. They hung him naked over a photo of Marie to make it look like he killed himself because of her."

"Where were you when all this was happening?" I ask, my question inadvertently lending credibility to his story.

"Asleep in my room. I'd had a few too many already that night and was sleeping it off."

"Right," I say.

"It's the truth, man!" Scooter insists.

I almost believe him, but say, "It will all get sorted out back in Paris. Better pack your bags."

He turns, looking dejected, and walks back to the Z Lounge. Before he gets there, the door swings open again. It's Brad. He waits for his friend to reach the door and then punches him in the face. Scooter doesn't go down. He swings back. Before long it's a brawl. Michi comes out and screams. Then she gets on her cell phone.

No honor among thieves . . . or murderers, I think, as I watch the brawl unfold. Then I hear sirens and see two HPD cruisers pull up in front of the lounge. Before long the brawl is over and each man is inside a cruiser.

I follow the cruisers to police headquarters on Beretania Street. When the officers unload Brad and Scooter, I'll be there. And then I'll catch up with my old pal Fernandez in homicide.

On the way to the station I remember Meighan telling me Scooter looked like he'd been drinking the night Ryan died. Then I become more convinced that Scooter has just told me the truth. And I kick myself for not checking out Kim's story that Heather had gone to the pharmacy that night. An internet search could have easily pulled up addresses and hours of pharmacies near 44 Rue de Écoles.

The case was not about the two buddies ganging up on Ryan. I fell for the obvious and missed some subtle clues. But I put the big pieces of the puzzle together. No doubt all the little pieces will soon fall into place too.

epilogue

I wish this case could have a happier ending. My finding the killers of Ryan Song will not bring him back to his grieving parents. But the torment leaves their faces when I tell them over a quiet dinner at their St. Louis Drive home that their son did not take his own life—that he paid with his life for standing up for what he believed in. I assure them that his heartless killers will be brought to justice.

"When we heard about you from the college," Mrs. Song says, "we knew if anyone could set things right about Ryan it was you."

I thank them for their confidence in me.

But what especially pleases me is the change in Mr. Song. When he rises from the table to say goodbye, he stands erect with a look of self-assurance in his eyes. He smiles through his pain with a smile that seems to come from deep within his heart. Nothing can ever compensate him for his loss, but he's no longer a broken man. His pride in his son and himself and his family has returned.

Mrs. Song stands at his side when I bid them *aloha*. She too manages a faint smile as she waves goodbye.

I was able to solve this case from the distance of seven thousand miles. I can't imagine ever having another case so far from Honolulu.

Looks like I've closed the book on Paris forever.

Part II
Another Problem in Paris

On a rain-slick street on the Left Bank a body lies in an expanding pool of blood, the lights of the Eiffel Tower reflecting on the darkened pavement.

A Good Samaritan runs into the street.

"Qu'est-ce qui s'est passé?" *Someone on the sidewalk asks her what happened.*

"Frappé par une voiture." *Struck by a car, she answers.* "Le conducteur ne s'est pas arrête." *The driver didn't stop.*

Soon the sirens of the Paris Police can be heard approaching.

The Good Samaritan feels the victim for a pulse. She looks up in anguish. "Mon Dieu!"

one

Monday, April 1. April Fools' Day. I'm in my Maunakea Street office in Chinatown facing a mound of tax forms and receipts. I hate paying taxes. And I hate even more coming up with figures to put on the forms. It's a kind of fiction, really, since I'm not the best record keeper. The question always in the back of my mind is: will the tax collectors buy it? I never know until I receive either a refund check from the Feds or a letter saying I'm being audited. The refund or audit letter from the state comes on Hawaiian time—later.

"April is the cruelest month," some poet said. I wonder if he was thinking about paying taxes.

I've got to take a break from these forms and figures. I step outside my office and glance at the hanging ten surfer airbrushed on my door and SURFING DETECTIVE: CONFIDENTIAL INVESTIGATIONS—ALL ISLANDS.

If only I had an investigation. I'd put off filing taxes until the April 15 deadline.

I walk down the hall by the shop of our resident psychic, Madame Zenobia. The odor of incense wafts into the hallway.

"Kai!" she shouts through her psychedelic bead curtain. "How about a quick reading? On the house."

"Sorry, Shirley"—Madame's real name is Shirley Schwartz—"I'm in kind of a hurry." That's a lie, but Shirley delving into my future means trouble. The news is either good and she's wrong, or bad and she's right.

"C'mon in. Won't take but a minute," she says. "Just got this new crystal ball yesterday from Amazon. Eight inches around. Cost only ninety-nine bucks. I love Amazon."

I peer into the candlelit incense haze. In her throne-like wicker chair Madame hovers over a large glass orb. My eyes smart. Crystal balls are a departure for Shirley. Her usual gig is reading palms and Tarot cards. I can't walk away now without seeming a heel. Plus I happen to know she's had a tough life. Her only son came home from Afghanistan in a box.

"Okay, if you can make it quick." Reluctantly I step in and sit. I gaze over the glinting orb at my office neighbor, her hair flaming red and frizzed, her mascara darker than a Hotel Street hooker's, and her beads and bangles more abundant than a gypsy's.

"Here we go." She bends down close to the crystal and puts both open palms around it, but doesn't touch the surface. The incense smoke makes it hard to see, hard to breathe. I'm waiting. And wary.

Shirley peers into the ball. Her face brightens. "I have it, Kai!"

"Tell me, Madame." I try not to sound too interested. "What's in my future?"

"A journey," she says.

"*A journey?* That's kind of generic, isn't it?" I thought I wouldn't care what she said, but this is a let-down. "The ball says nothing more specific?"

"Let me look again." Madame peers once more into the crystal. She moves her hands around the ball. "I see it now! I see it!"

"You see what?"

"You will travel far, Kai, to a foreign and exotic land."

I shake my head.

Madame looks annoyed. "Don't take your future lightly, Kai." She rises from her crystal ball. "The tendencies are strong."

"I've got no travel money," I say. "I don't even have a passport. Where could I go?"

"That will all be taken care of," she says. "Never mind the details. It will happen."

You see? This is why I don't like Madame Zenobia peering into my future. No way is what she's saying going to happen—which if it did might be a good thing—but now I have to worry about what the fortune might really mean, which is probably a bad thing. Either way is trouble.

"Thanks." I rise from my chair. "I'll send you a postcard from nowhere."

two

I pop downstairs to the *lei* shop beneath my office. Mrs. Fujiyama, the proprietor and my landlady, stands at her accustomed place behind the cash register ringing up a customer with three plumeria *lei*. The plumeria are cream white with yellow centers and I can smell their lemony perfume from here.

"'Morning, Mrs. Fujiyama," I say when the customer strides away.

She peers up at me over her half glasses. "Good morning, Mr. Cooke."

"Maybe I go *holoholo,*" I say, meaning to wander about.

"You go *holoholo?*" She seems surprised.

"Da Madame psychic upstairs," I point up, "say I going to journey far—to one foreign and exotic land."

"No listen to her, Kai." Mrs. Fujiyama makes a cuckoo gesture. "Da lady *lolo.*"

"Good. I staying hea. Mo' time fo' surf." I head out the door.

I step from the *lei* shop into the morning bustle of Chinatown. On this first day of April the sun beams down from the robin's egg blue sky. I'm hoping Shirley is wrong about my future. Now if we just get an early spring swell, today will be made. Let the future take care of itself.

I head for my parking garage. It's been said that most Chinatowns these days cater to tourists, but that is only part of the story here in Honolulu. Yes, there are curio shops where you can buy souvenirs and gizmos and gadgets, but you'll also find fishmongers, butchers, fruit and vegetable vendors, noodle makers, and many more purveyors of life's essentials. You may likewise encounter drug dealers, homeless people, and occasional rank odors wafting from empty storefronts, but it's all part of the flavor of this vibrant slice of the city.

I climb into my old Chevy, my surfboard riding inside next to me, and head for the uncrowded break near Point Panic called Flies. Usually I surf here with my buddy Kula, a rescued golden retriever, but I'm on the outs at the moment with his foster mom.

I'm about to pull my board from the car when my cellphone rings. Caller ID says PARADISE COLLEGE. I answer.

"Hello, Kai. Serena here." Serena Wright is Director of International Studies at the college. She's a bright Brit for whom I've done work before.

Suddenly I'm hopeful she has something new for me.

"Remember the sad case of Ryan Song?" She's referring to the murder of a study abroad student and surfer, an investigation I did not quite a year ago.

"Hanged in his own dorm room by his fellow students," I say. "How could I forget?"

"It's a miracle you solved that case in Paris without leaving Oʻahu."

"Hardly a miracle. But I appreciate the compliment." And now I'm wondering what that case has to do with her call. I don't have to wonder long.

"Kai, the college has another problem in Paris," Serena says. "It's a bit delicate and I'd prefer not to discuss it on the phone. Could you stop by my office straightaway this morning?"

I gaze at my surfboard and say, "How about in an hour or so?"

"It's actually a matter of some urgency," she says. "The sooner the better."

"Okay, I'll be there shortly."

I put away my phone and hit the waves.

Paddling out into the lineup I remember Madame's prediction. *Nah.* Even if Serena puts me on another problem in Paris, that doesn't mean I'm going there.

But I am curious.

three

After rinsing off in the public showers, I dress and head to the nearby campus of Paradise College.

Serena wastes no time launching into her problem. "Remember Marie Ho," she says, "the study abroad student who broke up with Ryan in Paris? She's the one you interviewed by email since she didn't return to Hawai'i with the others."

"Sure," I say. "She emailed me from Germany."

"That's her," Serena confirms. "Marie was traveling the continent with her new boyfriend, Pierre, the Sorbonne student she met in Paris."

And now I recall that Marie was an A-plus student who nonetheless got caught up in a cheating scandal in her French History course in Paris. The widespread cheating that Ryan resisted and reported to his professor led to the young man's death. I'm not sure Marie realized that at the time. She wasn't one of the ringleaders, but was naively swept along with her other classmates. At least that's the way it had appeared.

Serena continues: "It's been almost a year since Marie's semester abroad ended. She's dropped out of school and she hasn't come home. Her psychiatrist stepfather, Dr. Gordon Grimes, is concerned."

"Is she still traveling around Europe?" I ask.

"No, Marie returned to Paris shortly after your investigation and has been living there ever since. With Pierre, I understand."

"Why does her stepfather's concern matter to you? Or to the college?" I ask. "Isn't this something he could deal with himself?"

"That's what's delicate," Serena explains. "You see, the Ho Trust is a major donor to the college and it's awkward that Marie's dropping out and prolonged absence from home stem from her participation in the Study Abroad program."

"Awkward?" I say. "As in the college is worried the donations may stop flowing?"

"Exactly. Well, we don't know how much influence Dr. Grimes has with the Trust. His late wife, philanthropist Beatrice Ho, initiated the gifts more than a decade ago. Nonetheless, the college is anxious to appease Marie's stepfather in any way it can."

"And what's your opinion?"

Serena shakes her head. "My opinion is that Marie can do whatever she wants. She's twenty-one and certainly has enough money to do whatever she wants. But that's not the college's opinion. And I work for the college."

"So how can I help?"

Serena doesn't miss a beat. "Dr. Grimes would like to talk with you. He believes since you won Marie's trust during your investigation that you might be more effective in communicating with her than he has been."

"Sure. I could send her an email. I could call her."

Serena is quiet for a moment and then says: "Whatever the doctor wants, Kai. That's what the college wants."

"I doubt the doctor wants to hear about my investigation, since it doesn't reflect well on any of the students, including his brilliant stepdaughter."

"I don't expect he'll even ask you about Ryan," Serena says. "I'd consider it an enormous favor if you would talk with him. I'm confident he'll pay a consultation fee, but if he doesn't my office will."

"No worries," I say. "You've always taken care of me."

She writes the doctor's name and phone number on a sticky note and hands it to me. "I would appreciate it if you could arrange an appointment with him as soon as possible."

"I'll call him immediately," I say.

Before I leave I ask her to fill me in on Marie Ho. Serena tells me everything she knows, or at least everything she's willing and able to tell. Turns out the fun-loving A-plus student has had more than her share of sorrow. She lost not only her mother but also her father and brother, leaving her alone in the world except for her stepfather.

Back in my car I check the note Serena gave me. Dr. Grimes' name looks familiar, but I can't remember why. I call and he answers in a silky-smooth voice like in a TV commercial. It's an inviting and comforting voice that makes me feel in good hands. But my cynical side kicks in. If the stepdaughter cheated, even inadvertently, maybe the stepfather would too? As they say, "The fruit doesn't fall far from the tree."

But isn't that for blood relations, which Marie is not?

Still, I wonder.

four

I drive from the college through Waikīkī, pass Diamond Head, and motor into East Honolulu where in the distance Koko Crater soars. At the foot of the crater lies my destination, the ocean-side hamlet of Portlock.

The Ho residence on Portlock Road sits right on the water, hidden from the street behind a grove of palms. Across the flagstone driveway stretches a long impenetrable gate. I step out, speak into an interphone, hear that silky voice again, and then get buzzed through. The gate slowly opens and I drive in. The lushly landscaped grounds seem to roll on forever.

I step up to a grand entryway leading to carved *koa* doors and knock. From the thud of my knuckles the wood must be a half-foot thick. Before long the doctor appears. He's impeccably dressed, island-style, in a tasteful aloha shirt and linen slacks. His full beard reminds me of photos I've seen of legendary psychoanalyst Sigmund Freud.

Dr. Grimes leads me from a spacious foyer to an even more spacious living room, overlooking a swimming pool, fairway-sized lawn, and more palms framing the blue Pacific.

I try to start on a positive note. "Nice place you've got here."

"I've an apartment in town too," he says in those soothing tones, "but since my wife Beatrice died I have the pleasure of living here for the rest of my life. The oceanfront estate, of course, belongs to the Ho Trust."

"Must be a pleasure," I reply, but what I'm noticing more than the magnificent palace is how he hobbles along ahead of me with a cane.

"You notice my limp?" the doctor says as if he has eyes in the back of his head. "I was born with one leg shorter than the other. I wear this raised shoe," he points to his left foot, "and use this cane. It's nothing. I have overcome, as anyone who puts his mind to it can."

"Admirable, sir," I say.

Dr. Grimes gestures to two plush sofas on either side of a mango coffee table. He sits across from me and says out of the blue, "I'm an *active man*." He points to a mountain bike leaning against a living room wall. "I can pedal with anybody on Oʻahu," he says. *"Anybody.* I keep the bike in here because it's kind of expensive and it's my baby."

I gaze at his high-end bike and the term *compensation* comes to mind.

Then from the coffee table he picks up a model of a sleek racing boat. "Just like my 43-footer on Molokaʻi. This little missile cuts a swath across the water at one hundred miles per hour. I chose her name—Sea Ya Later—as a kind of joke. But it's true. Nobody can catch her."

"I bet you can cross the Molokaʻi Channel in no time, sir."

"Not anymore," he says. "She's still on the Friendly Isle, but in the hands of her new owner. After my wife Beatrice plunged from a sea cliff at Makapuʻu the ocean lost its allure for me."

"That would be Marie's mother?" I ask.

He nods. "Unfortunately, yes."

"I'm sorry, sir."

He waves his hand. "You didn't come here to talk about my late wife."

"No, sir, I came to talk about your stepdaughter."

He clears his throat. "As Ms. Wright probably told you, Marie went to Paris for the Study Abroad program. When the term ended she didn't come home. Nearly a year has gone by now."

"Have you asked her to return?"

"That's the problem. I'm having trouble getting in touch with her." The doctor slides to the edge of the couch. "She's fallen in with a phony artist who's draining her, but she can't see it. She's been sheltered all her life in the islands. This leech has another woman who may even be his wife. He's running some kind of sleazy *ménage à trois.*"

"*Ménage à trois?* You mean the three of them—doing it together?"

"The French." He raises his brows.

"What happened to Marie's Sorbonne boyfriend?"

"I'm talking about him—Pierre Garneaux. Only I doubt Pierre ever attended the Sorbonne. He was probably there just trolling for a woman like Marie—young and attractive and rich. She's the sole surviving heir of the Ho Trust. When she turned eighteen she started receiving her inheritance. She gets it all when she turns thirty-five or marries."

Hmmm. I'm startled by this different picture of Marie's boyfriend than I remember from the Ryan Song case.

"Here's a photo of the two of them on the Champs-Elysées." He hands it to me. "That's the Arch of Triumph in the background."

The young couple is standing on a wide and bustling Paris boulevard with the famous monument rising behind them. Pierre is long-haired, lean, and a head taller than Marie. She's nonchalantly smoking. Otherwise she resembles her college mugshot: bobbed hair, grey eyes, intelligent brow, and playful smile.

"Marie is going through money like water—ten to fifteen thousand euros a month," the doctor says. "That phony artist can't support his bohemian lifestyle in Paris on his shoddy work. They keep moving from place to place, probably because of his drugs and his women and his carrying on."

I'm curious about the figure. "How much in dollars is fifteen thousand euros?"

"Slightly more. Marie simply tells her bankers how much she wants and they wire it to her."

"With no limit?"

"Well, there's a theoretical limit since her money comes from interest and dividends from the Ho Trust, but she hasn't reached it yet."

"If you've not spoken with Marie lately, how do you know these things?"

"I've had reports from Paris. I'd go try to talk sense to her myself, but I'm not skilled at finding people who don't want to be found." Dr. Grimes pauses. "That's where you come in."

I recall Madame's prediction. *Again.*

The doctor produces an envelope on which is written one word: *Marie.* "I'd like you to deliver this envelope to her."

"In Paris?"

He nods.

"But . . . ." I consider the obvious: I've never been to Paris. I don't speak French. I'd get lost and couldn't even ask directions. Before I can air my concerns he addresses them.

"Ms. Wright has arranged for an interpreter and guide—an American professor fluent in French who knows the city well." Then the doctor sweetens the deal. "Your airfare, meals, and expenses will all be paid and your lodging provided by the college."

"When would you like me to go?"

"Immediately."

On that note I come up with a potential deal-breaker: "I don't have a passport."

Dr. Grimes grimaces, then says, "Let me call Ms. Wright."

He limps with his cane into an adjoining room. I can hear bits and pieces of a phone conversation. Then silence. And more conversation. After nearly ten minutes the doctor returns.

"Ms. Wright has made an appointment for you at the Honolulu passport agency at 4:15 pm this afternoon. You will need to take your airline ticket with you to prove urgency for an expedited passport. You can pick up the ticket from her before you go to the agency."

"Serena has my airline ticket already?"

"She was confident of your cooperation."

I look at my watch. "So I guess I better be going."

"Hold on." The doctor hands me the envelope with Marie's name on it. Then he pulls from a drawer in the coffee table a bundle of multicolored foreign currency bound with a rubber band. "This is for you."

"What is it?"

"Euros," he says. "For your trip."

"You and Serena have thought of everything," I say.

"Nothing left to chance." He smiles confidently. *"Bon voyage."*

Suddenly my future looks all too clear, even without the aid of Shirley's crystal ball.

five

Back inside my car I remove the rubber band from the euros. They're not gray-green like US dollars, but pink and yellow and purple and blue. Not the chiseled faces of Washington and Lincoln and Jackson but church spires and marble arches and quaint bridges spanning tranquil rivers. There's an assortment. I'm no math whiz and I don't count every last note, but I'd say conservatively there are a couple thousand in the bundle. If they're indeed worth more than dollars, my expenses will be well covered.

There's something else with the bills. A business card. It says, DR. GORDON J. GRIMES, MD. PSYCHIATRIST. PSYCHOTHERAPIST. And it gives his address at the Queens Hospital Physicians Building. I flip over the card. There's a note:

Mr. Kai Cooke:

The contents of the envelope are for Marie's eyes only. Ms. Wright assures me you can be trusted in this regard. Once you deliver the envelope, we will decide how to proceed from there.

GJG

I look more closely at the envelope. From its thickness I'd say it contains several sheets. It's one of those security-type business envelopes whose opaque blue interior hides what's inside. The back flap and ends are sealed with clear packaging tape.

Bullet proof. The doctor means what he says: "For Marie's eyes only."

I put the envelope and the euros in my glove box, start my car, and pull up to the gate. It opens as if by magic. In my rearview mirror I see Dr. Grimes in cycling gear mounting his bike. He pedals toward me, waves, and follows me out the gate. He turns right on Portlock Road and heads toward the surf spot called China Walls. He looks fit and vigorous riding his bike. No sign of his limp.

I drive back to Paradise College, per Dr. Grimes's instructions. Serena is waiting for me with a round-trip ticket to Paris, a city map, Metro pass, and a phrasebook and CD entitled *French for Travelers*. I glance at the airline ticket. Nearly three grand! My final destination is Paris CDG. I ask what CDG means and Serena tells me Charles De Gaulle. Then I notice the purchase date on the ticket. Yesterday.

I give Serena a look.

"I knew we could count on you, Kai." She looks a little sheepish—but not much. "And how could you resist a trip to Paris in April?"

"I couldn't," I respond. "Apparently it was in the cards."

"Of course, you'll be flying twice overnight—Honolulu to Newark and then Newark to Paris. There's no avoiding that."

"I'm a redeye veteran," I reply.

"These are *long* flights."

"No worries," I say, but then wonder if I should worry. My redeye flights have all been to the West Coast. Where everyone speaks my language.

Serena continues: "You're scheduled to be in Paris for one week, but your trip can be extended or shortened, depending upon when you deliver the envelope to Marie."

"So you know about the envelope?"

"Yes and no. I know about the envelope but I don't know what's inside."

"That makes two of us. But I assume a letter containing a sanitized version of what Dr. Grimes told me about Marie and Pierre."

"Safe assumption," she replies. "Anyway, you'll be staying at our student residence in the Latin Quarter at 44 Rue des Écoles. And you'll be escorted around Paris by the program's current resident director, Vivienne Stone. She's an associate professor of French who knows the city well. You'll like Viv. And I'm sure she'll like you."

"Vivienne? I knew a Vivienne from the college once—a long time ago. But her last name wasn't Stone."

"Stone is Vivienne's married name. I don't know her maiden name."

"Probably not the same woman," I say. "I think the Vivienne I'm speaking of must have left the islands."

After a few other details and preparations, plus Serena's kind offer of a ride to the airport the next day, I thank her and say goodbye.

"Wait," she says. "You'll need this confirmation number for your appointment this afternoon at the passport agency." She hands me a sheet with the number on it and other essential information. "Remember to bring along all required documentation, including two color photos. You have only one shot at this expedited passport. Or you will miss your flight tomorrow."

"I'll bring everything," I say, glancing at the sheet.

"Au revoir," she says.

I haven't heard that French phrase for nearly a year. It was on Ryan Song's suicide note—that he himself did not write. As he hung from a chandelier at 44 Rue des Écoles the note lay beneath him: *Au revoir, Marie.* Along with a photograph of her.

The young woman I'm flying over two oceans to find.

six

From Paradise College I drive to the Honolulu Passport Agency in the Prince Kuhio Federal Building on Punchbowl Street. I stop in first at a convenience store in nearby Restaurant Row that doubles as a passport photo studio. My mug is shot and within minutes two reasonable facsimiles of myself, in color, are returned to me in a handy little folder designed for the purpose.

Inside the passport office a surprisingly friendly agent greets me, looks over my forms, documents, and airline ticket and she says, "Lucky you—flying to Paris in April!"

"I'd rather stay here and surf," I say.

"Maybe because you've never been to Paris."

"How can you tell?"

"This is your first passport. You've never applied before."

She collects a couple hundred bucks from me—including an extra charge for expediting—writes some things on the various forms, excuses herself for a minute, then returns. "You can pick up your passport tomorrow morning after 10:00 am."

"That's it?" I'm surprised at how quickly it's all happened.

She nods. "Next stop Paris, France."

From the Federal Building I drive back to Maunakea Street, climb the stairs from the *lei* shop, and hurry past the incense haze wafting from Shirley's open door. Inside my office I reach over the tax receipts still piled on my desk to the phone. I call my attorney and musician friend Tommy Woo and break the news.

"Paris?" Tommy says. "Did you hear the one about the Frenchman who jumped into the river that runs through the city?"

"No, Tommy." There's no stopping his jokes.

"He was declared to be in Seine." Tommy explains, "Get it? That's in S-E-I-N-E."

"Thanks for the spelling lesson." I fill him in on the details of the case that I can share.

"So you're flying to Paris to deliver an envelope," he replies, "but you've never been to Paris and you don't speak French?"

"The college is setting me up with a professor to lead me around by the hand."

"A woman, I hope."

"Yes, a woman," I say, "with an all-too-familiar name."

"A long-lost love?"

"I'd rather not go into it."

Tommy rattles off more jokes about France. Where does he get them all?

"Gotta go." Hanging up is sometimes the only way to stop him.

"Wait, Kai. He sounds serious for a change. "Before you step on the airplane you've really got to listen to Sinatra singing 'April in Paris.'" Tommy starts crooning. He's no Sinatra.

I don't say so. Just, "Gotta go."

Despite myself, the next thing I do is open my laptop and watch a video of Old Blue Eyes' rendition of "April in Paris." Sinatra is obviously a pro at this, the way he moves on stage and works the crowd. The song is sentimental—filled with chestnuts in blossom and warm embraces of spring— but concludes on a somber, melancholy note. Sinatra asks plaintively what the city has done to his heart.

I doubt I'll be there long enough for Paris to even touch my heart. I close the video and go to Facebook, my surefire source for useful information about young people, and many older people too. I want to augment what Serena told me about Marie and to check on the credibility of Dr. Grimes' allegations about Pierre. I've never been asked before to hand-deliver an envelope. I served papers, of course. But those cases were in Honolulu, not in Paris.

Marie Ho's Facebook page has a shot of her silhouetted against the Paris skyline. Scrolling down I find some scant information about her. She studied at Paradise College— no mention of earning a degree—but no additional photos, no gallery of friends, etc. She apparently shares little with visitors who are not her Facebook friends. I could send her a friend request and hope she remembers me, but that's risky.

I don't find a Facebook page for a Pierre Garneaux. This is odd. From my experience, most people in their twenties wouldn't feel they existed without Facebook. So why not Pierre? Of course, he's French. I notice there is Facebook in the French language. But he's not there either.

Then I try a broader approach. I Google both Marie Ho and Pierre Garneaux. Not much more on Marie and almost nothing on Pierre. I try artists in Paris with the first name Pierre and come up with many, some living and some dead.

I find no living artist named Pierre Garneaux. But I do find one named Pierre LeTrois. The image of the tall, lean young man resembles the photo of Pierre Dr. Grimes gave me. There's a website and a blog with several paintings. Some Paris cityscapes and still-lifes and some nudes. The subject of most of the nude paintings, all signed by LeTrois, is a young dark-haired beauty whom I assume is also French. Is this the mistress or wife of the artist Dr. Grimes mentioned? *Lucky Pierre!*

Then I find one additional nude painting of a petite young woman who looks like the photos I've seen of Marie. Sunlight plays on her light brown hair—bobbed as in Marie's college mug shot. She's younger than the other woman, her figure almost girlish. Her expressive eyes are what strike me. They have the look of sadness but also of love—love, I assume, for the artist. Her gaze is very different from the abstract air of the darker model in the other paintings.

And finally here's a portrait of the artist himself in a slightly different style. A self-portrait?

I wonder why Pierre chose the pseudonym LeTrois. I plug the name into a French to English translator on my laptop. *LeTrois* means The Three. Is Pierre flaunting the fact that he has two beautiful lovers? A *ménage à trois?*

I wonder again about the French. I wonder again about Paris. And if I'm really up to this job.

seven

The next day, Tuesday, April 2, I pick up my shiny new passport, take care of a few last-minute details in my office, and rush back to my apartment to finish packing. Before long it's almost sunset and Serena is driving me to the airport. In my carry-on I've safely deposited the two items Dr. Grimes gave me: the sealed envelope for his stepdaughter and the bundle of euros for me.

"I'm forever grateful to you for taking this on," Serena says as we approach the terminal. "Whatever happens in Paris, the fact that you're going is what matters to the college. Even if you can't deliver the envelope to Marie, you're an ambassador for Dr. Grimes. And that's what he wants."

"He wants me to deliver the envelope," I say. "I'm absolutely sure of that."

"Of course," she says. "But have some fun while you're there. Viv will help you, I'm sure."

Viv? Vivienne? I wonder again about that name.

Checking in for my flight and displaying my new passport, I consider what Serena has just told me. I'm flying to Paris to deliver an envelope. For my trouble, I get a round-trip ticket, accommodation, a bundle of euros, and a friendly escort I may already know too well. And finally I'm encouraged, above all, to enjoy myself. Things could be worse.

I trudge through security and head to my gate. The departure lounge is flooded with the rich golds of sunset. The bulbous nose of a big Boeing almost touches the plate glass of the lounge. Serena told me I'm flying from Honolulu to Newark to Paris—two nights in the air through twelve time zones. *Hmmm.*

When my turn comes to board I make my way through the front of the airplane and see what I'm missing: first class passengers sipping champagne in leather recliners that tonight will transform into comfy beds. I squeeze into my narrower seat in the cramped economy cabin and prepare for a long ride. I pull from my carry-on *French for Travelers*. Maybe I can learn a little of the lingo over the next twenty-four hours?

Those hours go by achingly slowly.

Thursday, April 4, in the first light of dawn, another Boeing is descending over storybook farms and villages on the outskirts of Paris. After two overnight flights, and more than seven thousand miles traveled, I'm beat. But not too beat to take in the beauty of the French countryside.

The airplane touches down and parks at the futuristic international terminal at Charles De Gaulle Airport. I disembark, get my new passport stamped, collect my bag, and follow signs that say TAXI. I step outside and am surprised by the sharpness of the air. A temperature sign nearby reads 8 C. Mid-40s Fahrenheit, I'd guess. By Hawai'i standards, cold. I get goosebumps or, as we say in the islands, chicken skin.

The warm embrace of spring? Did Sinatra ever come to Paris in April? I slip on my light jacket, which does nothing. I didn't pack a hat or gloves since I own neither.

I hop into a Renault taxi, say *"Bonjour"* to the driver, and hand him a printed address Serena provided: 44 Rue des Écoles.

The driver says "Okay" and we speed off. The heater inside the Renault is cranked up. My chicken skin disappears.

After the gorgeous French countryside viewed from the air, the fringes of Paris seen on the ground look like any US city—a commercial and industrial district of office buildings, warehouses, and transportation and construction yards. Even graffiti. Big blue signs above the jammed expressway say "A-3" and "Paris–EST," which I take to mean the east side of Paris. The going is slow.

My phone rings. I'm surprised it works in France and I wonder how much it's going to cost me to take this call. I answer anyway. It's Dr. Grimes.

"Are you in Paris yet?" he asks.

"Yes, sir, I'm in a taxi heading into the city."

"How were your flights?" he asks, clearly as an afterthought.

"Long."

"Do you have the envelope with you?"

"At all times, sir."

"Good. Let me know as soon as you deliver it, or have anything to report," he replies. "Text is best. Anytime. Night or day. Don't worry about waking me."

"Will do," I say.

The doctor says goodbye. I'm not sure why he called. I don't think too hard about it. I don't question the motives of a client who gives me two thousand euros and a free trip to

Paris. Well, I do wonder why he would go to such extremes to get in touch with a stepdaughter who apparently has little interest in getting in touch with him.

The taxi slows to a crawl in the morning rush hour. The closer we get to the center of Paris, the slower we go.

When we finally descend into the city streets, I'm transported into what looks like a nineteenth-century movie set from *Les Misérables*: cream-colored stone buildings with wrought iron balconies, patina copper roofs, clay chimneys, and dormer windows. Not a skyscraper in sight. Sidewalk cafés sit on nearly every corner—patrons sipping coffee, smoking cigarettes, and huddling over newspapers called *Le Figaro* and *Le Parisien*. We pass bakeries and butcher shops and Metro stations. I roll down my window and hear church bells and whiff the pleasant aromas of baking bread and roasting chicken, and the more pungent odors of tobacco smoke and car exhaust and sweat.

The smells remind me of Honolulu's Chinatown, but with an alluring perfume of their own. There's no doubt. I'm in Paris.

The taxi crosses a wide grey-green river where low-slung barges and cruise boats steam by—the Seine Tommy joked about?—then traverses a bustling boulevard called Saint-Germain, and finally turns and stops across from 44 Rue des Écoles. The centuries-old townhouse looks just as I remember it from my case photos, in the same ornate style as the rest of Paris I've seen so far. Except balcony planters contain not one flower in bloom. The calendar may say April, but it feels like January.

Never mind. The place is hauntingly familiar. This is where Ryan Song died.

I hand sixty euros to the taxi driver, grab my bag, and cross Rue des Écoles. I ring a bell and the arched wooden door opens to an elderly French woman who I assume is the housekeeper.

She says, *"Bonjour,"* as if she's expecting me.

I repeat the word, again trying my fledgling French.

Once we get that out of the way, she escorts me onto a musty elevator and up three floors to a vacant student room. As soon as the door opens I know whose room it is. Or *was.* Ryan Song.

I glance at the chandelier from which the young Hawai'i surfer hung. The image of him there in board shorts, his ten toes dangling over the floor, is seared forever in my memory, even though I saw it only in police photos.

"La chambre est-elle satisfaisante?" the housekeeper says.

I think she's asking me if the room is okay, but I'm too jet-lagged and language deficient to do anything but nod.

She says, *"Merci,"* hands me the room key, and is gone.

I'm alone in the room. I walk toward a pair of tall French windows that in warmer weather would be open to those now barren planters and the gold-speared iron gates across the street of an august-looking institution called the Collège de France.

Instead of opening the windows I open my laptop and set it on the small table that was tipped over under Ryan's toes in the photos. I struggle with instructions provided in French for logging in to Wi-Fi, and then check my email. I have several new messages. One from Serena. Another from Tommy Woo: "Hey Kai, did you hear the one about the Paris prostitute who couldn't speak French?" Later. A bunch of junk mail. And one message from Professor Vivienne Stone.

I don't read much before I realize she's who I thought she was—only with a different last name.

Vivienne doesn't pretend not to know me. She says it will be wonderful to see me again. A lot has happened in the years since we first met. And she's anxious to catch up. Vivienne suggests we meet for lunch at a nearby café, Le Soufflot, after her morning classes. She says the café is close to Place du Panthéon—where I recall Marie was living with Pierre when Ryan died—and just a short walk from Rue des Écoles.

I email back that I will meet her at Le Soufflot at noon. I agree it will be wonderful to catch up after all this time. I'm not sure I really mean it. Will it be wonderful or painful? I fell for her back then as hard as I could fall. I had thought the feeling was mutual. I must have been wrong. Otherwise her last name might be the same as mine.

I try not to think about it. I'm dead tired and my only option to catch a wink before lunch, other than on the hardwood floor, is in a dead man's bed. I've never given much thought to crawling under the covers where a hanged man has slept, so I'm surprised how much it bothers me. But I climb in anyway and gaze up at the chandelier from which Ryan hung.

Recipe for a nightmare? Turns out I'm too sleep-deprived and jet-lagged to even dream.

eight

After an hour in Ryan's bed I'm awakened, groggier than before, by my phone's alarm. My body feels like lead. I can barely drag myself up. But I manage to shower, put on fresh clothes and the only jacket I brought, and then head to the café.

Consulting my Paris map, I walk barely a block along Rue des Écoles to a busier street called Rue Saint-Jacques and then stroll through the heart of the University of Paris, the Sorbonne. The campus has more domes and columns and archways than I've ever seen in one place before. The air is still chilly so I pick up my pace.

April's warm embrace? Chestnuts in blossom? I see only bare trees. Not a single green bud. An old Frenchman, cigarette dangling from his lip, trudges by in a thick wool overcoat. He's not fooled by romantic notions about April in Paris. He lives here. He knows.

I shove my hands deep into my pockets and keep walking. Rue Saint-Jacques soon intersects Rue Soufflot, a wide sloping street lined with cafes, bookstores, and tourist shops. At the summit of Rue Soufflot looms the Panthéon, under whose lofty dome lie some of France's most illustrious intellectuals, artists, revolutionaries and patriots. Or so my tourist map says. But like Sinatra's song, the famous landmark isn't living up to its hype. Its dome is shrink-wrapped in white plastic and surrounded by scaffolding—looking about as majestic as a corn silo.

With the Panthéon under wraps behind me I hike down to the corner café. Under an orange awning emblazoned LE SOUFFLOT clear plastic curtains shield sidewalk diners from the cold. But there aren't any diners on the sidewalk that I can see. The lunch crowd must have retreated to the comparatively warmer comfort of the café proper. I draw open one of the curtains and step under the awning. Half a dozen gas heaters glow above little round tables.

I was wrong. There is one diner under the heater's glow. She's sitting alone, bathed in cold sunshine streaming through the curtains. She's in black with an elegant blue-green scarf setting off her strawberry hair.

I walk toward her and she gives me her warm hand. Mine, to her, must feel like ice.

"Hello, Kai," Vivienne says in her silvery tones I remember so well. "Long time."

"Hello, Vivienne." I sit down across from her, taking in the lovely rose petal scent of her perfume.

"I thought you wouldn't mind sitting here," she says, her hazel eyes still brimming with the charisma that captivated me back then. "I remembered you prefer the outdoors. You being a surfer and all."

"You remember right."

Then I notice the rock on her ring finger. It's a big one.

"You're no longer Duvane?"

"No, it's Stone now," she says. "How about you, Kai? Still solo?"

"Yes." I hesitate. "Well, I've dated on and off."

"And at the moment—are you on or off?"

"Off."

Her smile warms. Is she toying with me?

I try to move us along. "Mr. Stone is a lucky man."

"Professor Stone," she corrects me. "I talked with Jeremy on the phone last night."

"Did your husband stay back in Hawai'i?"

"No, he's at Princeton now." She looks slightly pained. "Jeremy left Paradise College last term. We've been living apart since then."

"Sounds inconvenient," I say.

"I can't begin to tell you."

The waiter arrives. Here's one promise of Paris that doesn't disappoint. He's the perfect picture of a French waiter: white shirt, black vest and bow tie. Silver tray in one hand, white napkin in the other. And a pencil-line mustache. *The real thing.*

"Bonjour!" he says. *"Que voudriez-vous?"*

Vivienne responds, *"Deux vins chauds, s'il vous plaît."* Then to me, her smile returning, "You'll love this, Kai. Hot mulled wine on a chilly day. The French don't often drink *vin chaud* with lunch, but it will help you thaw out."

When the waiter hands us menus and departs I say, "I'm sure I'll love the hot wine if you don't mind a sleepy lunch partner. I've got jet-lag like you wouldn't believe."

"I would believe," she says. "I've done those two overnight flights. They're killers."

We scan our menus. Vivienne suggests Le Soufflot's famous omelets. Soon the waiter returns with a baguette and two glasses of steaming red wine in which float orange slices and cinnamon sticks. I can smell the spicy aroma even before he sets the glasses down. He takes our orders and again departs.

Vivienne proposes a toast. "To your April in Paris. And to my happy surprise at meeting you again."

"And to mine at meeting you."

We both sip. The hot wine instantly rolls through my body.

"I don't usually drink at lunch," I say.

"Oh, you should," Vivienne replies, "at least while you're here. A glass of wine in a Paris café is one of life's pleasures. You see, Kai, you sit in a café and you sip and you watch the world go by. The more you sip, the better the world looks. Until it's a wonderful world and you're happy to be in it. You stop trying to solve the world's problems and your own problems and you start living."

"*You*—problems?" I ask, the wine already loosening my tongue.

"Everybody's got problems," she replies. "But the wine helps."

I sip again and peer through the curtains onto Rue Soufflot. "I see what you mean. It is a wonderful world out there. Even if it's a cold world."

"Oh, it will warm up," she says. "By the end of April."

"I'll be gone long before then," I reply. "Unless this case takes an unexpected turn."

The waiter arrives with our lunch. The scrumptious omelets hang over the edges of our plates, oozing melted cheese. And these french fries! Do they cook them in duck fat? *Unreal.* I'm grateful lunch is moving along. Because the more I sip hot wine, the more I wish for the way things used to be between Vivienne and me.

I turn our conversation to the case. "What can you tell me about Marie Ho?"

"Marie was my student at Paradise College," Vivienne replies. "I'm sure you've heard she's bright and effervescent, but you should know her apparent zest for life covers a great deal of sadness and pain."

"Serena mentioned her misfortunes," I say, but keep to myself her succumbing to the cheating I uncovered in the Ryan Song case.

"Marie can be dark and gloomy sometimes, but I guess that comes with the territory. You see, her father and her brother both died when she was a teenager. A few years later her mother—an admirable woman and a major donor to the college—plunged from a cliff at Makapu'u. Mrs. Ho was apparently visiting the site where her son lost his life in a surfing accident. Whether she fell or jumped, it was a terrible blow to Marie."

"That's a lot of sorrow for a young woman to bear."

"Marie is vulnerable, but she's also tough," Vivienne replies. "She's got a granite streak that's helped her survive."

"Then maybe her stepfather shouldn't worry about Pierre, or anybody, leading her around by the nose?"

"I doubt Dr. Grimes knows her well," Vivienne says. "I don't think they're close. When Marie started college she opted to live on campus rather than with him."

"Then why is he trying so hard to get in touch with her?" I ask.

"Perhaps he's concerned about something else?"

"Well, he did tell me that most of her money goes to Pierre, who the doctor claims is a phony artist and a Sorbonne pretender."

"You could find out if Pierre graduated, or even attended, from Pénélope Constant, Director of International Studies at the University. I'll introduce you."

"I'd appreciate that."

"I'm here to help," Vivienne says. "You have me tomorrow, Friday, until my afternoon appointment. On Saturday I'm leading a student excursion to Versailles. Want to come?"

"Sure, if I deliver the envelope to Marie on Friday. Otherwise, on Saturday I'll keep trying. Solo."

"Okay. Shall we meet tomorrow at Place du Panthéon about ten?"

"Ten is good," I say.

Lunch eventually wraps up and we're about to say goodbye when I can't help asking, "Is Jeremy why I never heard from you again?"

Vivienne gets that pained look again. "You'll never know how sorry I am, Kai." Her voice deepens. "I guess I thought it would be kinder if I just sort of faded away."

"Well, I did wonder."

I head back to Rue des Écoles, the haunting strains of Vivienne's voice following me. The air is still nippy. Shafts of cold sunlight slant between buildings. I doubt she's as sorry as I am that she just faded away.

Back in Ryan Song's room I flop onto his bed. Why didn't I ask Vivienne about moving to another room? I'm so tired now it hardly matters. Tonight I'll sleep like a dead man.

When night finally comes, the lights of Rue des Écoles cast a ghostly shadow of the chandelier against the wall. I wake up several times to the image of Ryan hanging there.

I rub my eyes. I must be seeing things.

nine

Friday morning, April 5, I awake before my alarm goes off. I shower and dress, grab the envelope, and step along the sidewalk toward the aroma of baking bread. The baguettes, croissants, and gorgeous pastries in the shop windows of a corner *boulangerie* prompt me to consult my *French for Travelers.* Yes, the word means bakery. Before long I'm sipping French roast coffee, munching a buttery croissant, and recalling how I met Vivienne.

I was at a party at a Paradise College professor's home— Serena must have invited me—when I spotted a tall, willowy redhead captivating a gaggle of guys. When one guy stepped away to refresh his drink I took the opening to introduce myself.

Her name was Vivienne Duvane—an assistant professor of French. She explained in her rich tones that she was writing a book on George Sand.

"I've heard of him," I proudly replied.

"Her," she corrected me.

We soon established that I surfed and she wanted to. We made a date for the next morning in Waikīkī. She showed up with her trim athletic body adorned in a bikini that left me nearly speechless. I managed to give her a brief ground school on the beach and then we got in the water. We joked and laughed. Already we were clicking.

"I'll show you what a woman can do," she said and then stood up on her very first wave. *Totally stoked.*

On her second wave she tumbled in and didn't pop up. I dove down for her. When we surfaced together—facing each other—our lips brushed. That's all it took. The next wave drenched us. We didn't care.

I finish my coffee, check the envelope in my pocket, and hike up a side street called Rue Valette that perfectly frames the Panthéon. I'd marvel at the grand dome, but it's still wrapped in plastic and surrounded by scaffolding.

Strolling up the narrow street I recall that after the surf lesson Vivienne and I went out every night for the next week. Then she told me she had won a yearlong research fellowship in Brussels. Within days I was driving her to the airport. We said our tearful goodbyes and vowed to stay in touch.

I did. She didn't.

After her first few weeks away I never heard from her again. My pride was hurt. I had no idea I was so forgettable.

I reach Place du Panthéon and circle around. When I find Vivienne she smiles warmly and looks glad to see me. I may be imagining that. After we exchange pleasantries—"How did you sleep?" "Don't ask"—we get down to business.

Our first stop is the Hôtel Place du Panthéon where Pierre and Marie—and maybe the other woman—shared an apartment. If Dr. Grimes is correct about their moving constantly, I doubt they are still there. But maybe someone in this small hotel knows where the pair, or the trio, went.

The Hôtel Place du Panthéon sits shoulder to shoulder with two other boutique hotels with nearly identical wrought iron balconies and French windows.   A nattily-dressed doorman stands in front of two potted evergreens flanking the glass doors.   The lobby of gleaming marble, colorful bouquets, and plush period furniture suggests room rates well above what a typical college student or even recent gradate might afford.   Behind an elegant cherry desk sits a French woman in a stylish dark suit.

"Bonjour!" She smiles when we approach.

I turn to Vivienne who launches into a beautiful blur of French.   I relish the melodious sounds of the language in her voice, but can pick out only a few words, such as Marie and Pierre.

The clerk's smile fades when she realizes we are not prospective guests, but returns when she speaks of Pierre.

Vivienne explains: "She remembers Pierre fondly and says he rented an apartment himself before Marie joined him."

I wonder how Pierre was paying. If Dr. Grimes is correct, maybe the impoverished Pierre was not only using drugs, but also selling them?   Or did the other woman pay?

"Was another woman living with them?" I ask Vivienne, who conveys the question to the clerk.

Vivienne translates her answer: "Yes, from time to time there was another woman—Pierre's sister."

His *sister?* A convenient French way to explain a *ménage à trois*?

"Who paid the rent after Marie moved in?" I ask.

"Pierre," Vivienne translates the full reply.   "And that's odd.   He's still paying but the clerk hasn't seen them for months."

"Where is his apartment?" I ask. "Can we see it?"

"On the second floor, number twenty-four," Vivienne responds, "but since the apartment is rented she says we can't go in. She would be happy to show us a similar room that is unoccupied."

"Tell her thank you," I say, eyeing a nearby circular stairway. "Maybe we can just have a look ourselves?"

Vivienne follows my eyes up the stairs and says: "That staircase most likely leads to the dining room. I doubt she would object to us seeing it."

Vivienne asks and confirms.

"Please tell her many thanks," I say.

Vivienne does and then I add, *"Merci."*

We climb the circular stairs past the dining room to the second floor and follow a burgundy and cream carpet to room twenty-four. The room is locked. I knock, but no one answers. Down the hall a cleaning cart stands outside an open door.

I step to the cart, Vivienne behind me, stick my head in the door and say, *"Bonjour."*

A chambermaid moving a feather duster over an antique gold mirror replies with the same. And then, *"Puis-je vous aider?"*

I turn to Vivienne. "Ask her if she can show us room twenty-four."

My guide gets what sounds like the same response we received from the desk clerk. Vivienne shakes her head.

"Let's try this," I say. I open my wallet and scan the multi-colored assortment of euros I put there. First I reach for a baby blue twenty, and then reconsider. I pull a mint-green one hundred, hand it to the chambermaid, and trot out my fledgling French, *"S'il vous plaît."*

"Oh, Monsieur!" she says with a startled look. *"Merci! Merci!"* She pulls a plastic passkey card from her apron, turns toward room twenty-four, and says, *"Allons-y,"* which Vivienne translates as, "Let's go."

As we follow she winks at me. "Good job."

"Just the basic tools of private investigation," I respond. "Which seem to work as well in Paris as in Honolulu."

The chambermaid opens the door to a spacious room with a balcony overlooking the Panthéon under wraps. The decor is elegant like the lobby. My eyes are drawn to the bed— huge by France's or any nation's standards. I can imagine three young people playing in that big bed. But it doesn't look like the room has been used in that way lately. More like a studio or a gallery.

Everywhere are paintings—unframed oils on canvas. One of the Panthéon, minus plastic wrap. But most of nudes, with the monument in the background. Some paintings are on easels. Some stacked against walls. Most are signed Pierre LeTrois. I recognize a few from Pierre's website—the one of the young local Hawai'i beauty in a provocative pose on a beach. And a few of the other woman.

Vivienne scans the paintings. Her voice rises in pitch. "These are quite good."

"Really?" I ask, remembering Dr. Grimes's notion that Pierre was a pretender.

"Yes," she says. "I think so. The nudes remind me of Manet's *Olympia* and some of Seignac's work. They're not that good, of course. But promising."

"Sounds like you know something about French art," I say. "So maybe you can tell me this: Would a French artist's own sister pose for him naked?"

"Why not? If she loves her brother and wants to help his work along. Maybe she was flattered?"

"Or maybe she isn't his sister?" I reply. "Maybe she's his lover?"

"I'm not convinced Pierre painted every canvas," Vivienne says. "The styles are different. Perhaps the apartment might be used by another painter?"

The chambermaid is starting to fidget. I guess she could get in big trouble if she's caught letting us into an already rented apartment.

I sense we better wrap this up, but first I ask Vivienne to ask the chambermaid if the threesome used or sold drugs.

The woman shrugs.

"What did she think of Pierre?" I ask. "Did she like him?"

This brings a smile to the chambermaid's face and she becomes voluble. Vivienne turns to me. "She says he was a very nice young man—always kind and courteous and generous to her. Some tenants are rude or arrogant. Not Pierre. She wishes they were all like him."

I try again. "Does she know why they left the paintings and continue to pay rent?"

"The chambermaid says," Vivienne replies, "Pierre yearned to live in Montmartre."

"Where?"

"Montmartre," Vivienne explains. "It's a hillside bohemian community of artists—or used to be—on the northern edge of Paris. Picasso, Renoir, Monet, and even Van Gogh once lived and worked there. Today's starving artists can't afford Montmartre. They can't afford this address either."

"But Pierre can—on Marie's money?"

"On somebody's money," my guide replies.

"Does she have any idea where in Montmartre they moved?"

Vivienne translates and the chambermaid shakes her head.

"An address? A street?"

"She says to try around *Le Bateau-Lavoir* studio where Van Gogh and later Picasso painted."

I say to the chambermaid, *"Merci beaucoup."*

She bows and says, *"De rien."*

I don't know what that means, but I do know we have a new lead.

ten

As we step from the hotel onto Place du Panthéon, a grey French car pulls up and a male passenger jumps out and hustles into the hotel. What's his hurry? The driver leaves the motor running.

"What kind of car is that?" I ask Vivienne.

"Citroën," she says. "Why?"

"I'm curious about this Citroën. Probably because of the man dashing into the hotel."

While the driver is preoccupied, I step behind the car and look at its license plate. I've never seen a French plate up close before. It's long and narrow, compared to American plates, with two vertical bands of blue on either side, and letters and numbers in the middle. On a hunch I take a photo of the plate with my phone.

Vivienne and I then circle the Panthéon on foot and hike down a few blocks to a Metro stop on Boulevard Saint-Germain called Maubert-Mutualité. Near the station the earthy aroma of a farmer's market wafts our way. Under the bustling open-sided tents I feast my eyes on the reddest tomatoes and the greenest beans I've ever seen. I take a deep breath, inhale the aroma, and feel for the first time I'm fully awake.

We take stairs down into the Maubert station, produce our Metro passes, and descend further into the musky underground. Before long a high-pitched squeal turns my head to an approaching train whose marquee says BOULOGNE/ PONT DE ST-CLOUD. The cars roll to a stop, doors clank open, and passengers pour out toward green signs that say SORTIE.

"That's us," Vivienne says and we step aboard and wedge into a narrow seat for two. The train pulls away from the station and accelerates into the darkness. The electricity on the train is not limited to its motors. I haven't been this close to Vivienne for years.

We take two more trains to the Blanche station at the foot of Montmartre. We climb into a chestnut-lined median on Boulevard de Clichy where the bare chestnuts, despite Sinatra's song, are not yet in blossom. Across the boulevard looms the red windmill of the famous cabaret Moulin Rouge. *Moulin,* Vivienne tells me, means windmill and *rouge* of course means red. Behind us in what she calls the Pigalle district sex shops—block after block of them—radiate a neon glow. It's barely noon and still nippy, but sidewalks around the sex shops are teeming.

We cross Boulevard de Clichy and hike up a sloping foothill street called Rue Lepic and into cobblestone lanes that were once home to renowned artists. If the chambermaid at Hôtel Place du Panthéon is right, this is where Pierre Garneaux, a.k.a. Pierre LeTrois, yearned to live.

We have no address. That's never stopped me from finding anyone before. But this will be my first time in Paris. My plan is to show Marie's and Pierre's photos around until I'm able to find someone who can identify them and tell me where they live. Once we reach the *Bateau-Lavoir*. Whatever that is.

We huff past bakeries, bars, wine merchants, fruit stands, brasseries, and souvenir shops displaying postcards of a big white church atop the hill that Vivienne calls the Basilica of the Sacred Heart, or *Sacré Coeur*. And she explains that Montmartre for much of its history was outside city limits and a notorious hangout of rebels, revolutionaries, bohemians, artists, and prostitutes. I wonder out loud if that's why the Moulin Rouge and all those sex shops are here. She says Montmartre has always been the place where respectable Paris comes to play.

"That's Dr. Grimes's view of Pierre," I said. "Enjoying every pleasure at Marie's expense."

"Marie's stepfather may be prejudiced against her French boyfriend."

"Can't wait to meet him myself," I say. "I'm more than curious about our lucky Pierre."

"Me too," she replies. "Lucky Pierre, indeed."

We climb a few more blocks and turn into a cobblestone lane of lively open-air cafés and bars. Customers scurry under cover as it starts to drizzle. Umbrellas sprout like wild mushrooms. We have no umbrella. I flip up the hood of my light jacket and Vivienne does the same with her coat. The rain makes the chilly air feel even colder.

I glance behind us. A grey Citroën is moving slowly—the same Citroën that pulled in front of the Hôtel Place du Panthéon? And the same two men inside? I check the plates against the photo in my phone. My hunch was right.

How did they find us? We traveled underground on the Metro. Our destination was known only to us. Well—and also to the chambermaid at Hôtel Place du Panthéon. She was willing enough to break rules for us for one hundred euros. Would she spill where we were headed for even less?

"Remember those two men in the Citroën at Place du Panthéon?" I say to Vivienne. "They're here."

"Should we be concerned?" she asks.

"If they mean us harm," I reply, "I doubt they would show themselves so openly."

"Strange. Why are they following us?"

"At this point I can only guess. Are they after Marie? Or the envelope with her name on it? Or have they nothing to do with the case? And then I wonder out loud, "Vivienne, any reason they would be following you?"

"Me?" Her color rises. "I'm an American professor teaching American students in Paris. What would a couple of Frenchmen want with me?"

"I'm just asking," I say, surprised by her seeming overreaction. "Maybe I shouldn't have."

"You should," she says. "We need to be honest with each other, Kai."

Why suddenly, after years of our being out of touch, is honesty between us so important to her? I don't ask.

The Citroën stays a half block behind us. We turn onto a rain slick street called Rue Ravignan that climbs straight up the hill.

"If we're really being followed," Vivienne says, "they'll need to hop out now and walk. Where we're going is footpath only."

"Good. We may lose them."

As Vivienne and I hike in the drizzle she explains that Rue Ravignan leads to the *Bateau-Lavoir* studio. "This is a place to which a budding artist like Pierre might gravitate."

Soon we reach a footpath called Place Emile Goudeau and a small storefront displaying reproductions of paintings by artists associated with Montmartre. The studio itself, Vivienne explains, is behind the storefront.

"Le Bateau-Lavoir means the laundry boat," she says. "In Picasso's time the building was dark and dirty and rickety, swaying and creaking in stormy weather, reminiscent of washing boats on the Seine. Despite this, Picasso painted one of his most noted pieces here—*Les Demoiselles d'Avignon*, The Ladies of Avignon—considered a pivotal work of the Cubism movement."

"Impressive," I say, referring more to her knowledge of Picasso than to the painting itself.

I look behind us. No Citroën. One or both men could be on foot, lurking around the next corner.

I pull out my photos of Marie and Pierre. The image of the carefree young couple together jars with the doctor's appraisal of Pierre, and seems more in line with the different picture of him emerging here in Paris.

To find missing persons in Honolulu I might open my laptop and search trusted databases. Here in Paris, not knowing the language makes that difficult, though I'm sure Vivienne would assist if I ask. So I stand upslope from the *Bateau-Lavoir* and show the photos to any passerby who will look. If Marie and Pierre really do live here, I'm banking that someone sooner or later will recognize them.

Vivienne asks each prospect, *"Connaissez-vous ces personnes?"*

I strike out with one and then another. Then nearly a dozen. Until a middle-aged man with an umbrella says, *"Ah, Pierre. Oui."*

Vivienne asks if he knows where Pierre lives.

He responds, points up the hill, and moves on. Vivienne explains the man said that the couple lives on the curving stretch of Rue Ravignan immediately above us.

We go there. Large homes line either side of the hillside street. There may be several apartments inside each. How to find Marie and Pierre in them? I can knock on doors. But I ask Vivienne, just in case, if she knows a better way.

"What I would do to find someone in Paris," she explains, "is log on Yahoo.fr and type pagesblanches.fr, then enter Paris, and the person's name."

"I should have asked sooner." I shake my head.

"Well, I thought you had your own methods."

"I do, but next time don't hesitate to suggest."

"Okay." She pulls a small tablet from her purse, logs in, and inputs the name Pierre Garneaux.

We wait while the database searches. Close matches, but no hit.

"Any other ideas?" I ask.

"One other possibility," she says. "Instead of typing Paris in the city field, I'll put IDF, or Île de France, in the district or region field. This will search for Pierre in Paris and its suburbs."

She does this. We wait. The search turns up more near matches, and our Pierre Garneaux himself in Place du Panthéon. In other words, we've struck out.

"We can also try posting an MC—missed connection—on Paris Craigslist. We'd have to hope that they see it and then respond. But if they are trying to keep a low profile, they may be suspicious and not respond. Even if they answer, it would probably take time."

"Wait," I say. "Search your database again using the name Pierre LeTrois."

She does.

Voilà! An address in Montmartre on Rue Ravignan pops up, only steps from where we are. It's a modern buff brick apartment building of about six stories that curves around the bend in the road and overlooks *Le Bateau-Lavoir*. The perfect place for a budding artist.

The wrought iron gates at the entrance are locked tight. No surprise. A keypad would allow entrance if we had a code. We don't. We could try to trail a resident in, but on this quiet street it would look all too obvious.

I hear a click above us and the sound of a sliding glass door opening. On the second floor a woman steps onto her balcony.

"Bonjour!" Vivienne looks up.

The woman gazes down at us in the drizzle and replies, *"Bonjour."*

Then Vivienne starts into a spiel.

"Oui." The woman responds. Good sign? And then speaks rapidly.

Vivienne asks for clarification, as if she's puzzled. The woman replies.

"Does she know Pierre and Marie?" I ask.

"Yes, they were her neighbors."

"*Were* her neighbors?"

"They moved a few weeks ago."

"Where did they go?" Maybe Dr. Grimes was right about their vagabond lifestyle?

Vivienne asks and then reports, "She's not sure. One of her neighbors said they moved to Rue Saint-Dominique, near the Eiffel Tower, above the restaurant of a popular chef. But she can't remember the name of the chef or the restaurant."

"Why did they move?" I ask.

"She doesn't know," Vivienne replies, "but was sorry to see them go—Pierre, Marie, and Nicole."

"Were they lovers? The three of them?" I feel compelled to test Dr. Grimes' claim.

"Oh, monsieur, je ne sais pas," the woman replies. I can almost figure this one myself. The woman says she wouldn't know.

"Ask if she ever saw Pierre painting."

"Oui," she says again. Vivienne explains that Pierre showed the woman a painting of the *Sacré Coeur*. She claims it was beautiful."

"Did he show her any nude paintings? Any of all three of them together?"

"Non, monsieur," she says again.

Vivienne thanks her and we step away from the apartment building.

"Why would a young and promising painter who yearned to live in Montmartre, steeped in the artistic traditions of Picasso and Van Gogh, move to a busy tourist district in the shadow of the Eiffel Tower?"

The words are barely out of my mouth when I see the grey Citroën around the bend on Rue Ravignan—both men inside the car again.

"Do you have time to go with me to Rue Saint-Dominique?" I ask Vivienne.

"Sorry, Kai, I have that appointment this afternoon." She perks up. "But tell you what, I'll show you Rue Saint-Dominique and explain how to get there."

"How will you do that if you can't go with me?"

"The *Sacré Coeur*." She points to the big white church atop the hill. "From there you can see all of Paris."

eleven

We walk up Rue Ravignan around a bend where the Citroën is parked. The two men inside see us coming and look straight ahead. Do they think we haven't noticed them? Do they think they're invisible?

When we come up on the Citroën I almost bang on a window and shout, "Why are you following us?" In English, of course.

I let the temptation pass. We leave the Citroën behind. Having them think their cover isn't blown may work in our favor. If they watched us interview the woman in the balcony on Rue Ravignan they will no doubt get to her as they probably got to the chambermaid at the Hôtel Place du Panthéon. So I may have company on Rue Saint-Dominique.

As we hike up to the big white church the drizzling stops, but flinty grey clouds still span the horizon. There's not a trace of blue. I glance over my shoulder, looking for the Citroën. I don't find it. Did they give up? Or are they already talking to the woman on Rue Ravignan?

We keep climbing. Before long the massive central dome of the basilica at the top of the hill comes into view.

It's a grand church—startlingly white and dominating—with several smaller domes surrounding the central dome.

"Even though we don't have time for the full tour," Vivienne says, "you should at least step inside."

"Okay. I may not be back this way again." I follow Vivienne in.

The church is enormous, cold, and dim. Not to mention slammed with sightseers. You'd think so many warm bodies admiring murals and statuary and stained glass would warm a place. But not even the flickering votive candles—hundreds of them—seem to help.

As I'm taking in the chilly magnificence, Vivienne excuses herself and quietly steps into a row of pews near the altar. She kneels, crosses herself, and puts her palms together. Her strawberry hair picks up the faint glow of the omnipresent candles. I gaze at the ceiling above the altar to a mosaic in sapphire and gold of Jesus's uplifted and welcoming arms.

After a while I look down again. Vivienne rises, crosses herself again, and walks toward me. Her eyes are glistening.

"Is everything alright?" I've never seen her cry before.

She nods, produces a tissue, and wipes her eyes. "So, would you like me to show you Rue Saint-Dominique?" Her voice is husky. "And how to get there?"

"Absolutely," I say. "If you feel up to it."

We do an about face and backtrack through the church. I'm not noticing the cold so much now or the crowds. I'm wondering about Vivienne. Why was she crying? And not talking about it? *Everybody's got problems,* I recall her saying.

Outside the sky remains grey, but no rain.

People are milling about on a terrace fronting the basilica and overlooking the city. Under the blanket of clouds we can see for miles. We squeeze into an open spot along a parapet and take in the view. Paris' magical skyline stretches out before us.

I vaguely recognize the panorama—though I've never been here before—from old movies where lovers gaze into each other's eyes while Paris lies enchantingly at their feet.

"Romantic, isn't it?" Vivienne's musical tones return. She points into the far distance. "There. Over on the right. Do you see it?"

"See what?" I follow her finger. In the far reaches of the view I spot what looks like a needle pointing into the sky. "That?"

"The Eiffel Tower," she says, her tears gone now. "That's where you're going. Rue Saint-Dominique begins barely a block from the tower."

"Having a landmark should help," I say.

Vivienne looks doubtful. "I feel bad about abandoning you."

"No worries," I hear myself say. "I'll find my way. After all, I am a detective."

"I could help you plan your route tonight. We could spread out the map and go over it together."

"Thanks, but I've got this envelope to deliver and I can't afford to waste the afternoon."

"No need to waste the afternoon," she says. "Why don't we ride back together to Maubert-Mutualité and I'll arrange for you to see Pénélope at the University of Paris?"

"See who at the university?"

"Pénélope Constant," Vivienne says. "Remember I told you she's the Director of International Studies? She could tell you if Pierre was enrolled at the Sorbonne and maybe pass along other useful information."

"You talked me into it," I reply, secretly relieved. I pull out my phone and see that I'm getting a strong signal on the summit of Montmartre.

"Do you mind?" I say. "I need to ask Marie's stepfather a question."

"Kind of early in Honolulu, isn't it?"

She's right. It's barely afternoon in Paris, which means the wee hours of the morning in the islands.

"He said to text or call any time," I explain. "Maybe he silences his cell phone at night?"

"Go ahead," she says. "I'll take in the view."

I text Dr. Grimes: "Making progress. Uncovered two recent addresses for Marie today. Going to a third tomorrow, envelope in hand. Am being followed. Any idea who or why?"

On the Paris Metro we backtrack from Blanche to Maubert-Mutualité and climb again into chilly Boulevard Saint-Germain. The farmer's market is closed now. Only the empty tents remain.

Vivienne pulls out her cell phone and calls Pénélope Constant. I hear my name mentioned in Viv's melodious French. After a while she says, *"Merci, Pénélope! Merci!"*

A good sign.

"You're all set," she says. "Pénélope can see you if you can get there within thirty minutes."

"I can get there," I say.

Vivienne checks her watch. "Oops, I've got to rush to my appointment." But first she gives me directions to Pénélope's office. We agree to meet this evening at Chez René, a Boulevard Saint-Germain bistro. I thank her and watch her stride up a long and sloping street called Rue Monge.

Then I walk through Place du Panthéon to the University. Following Vivienne's directions I arrive at a small building plastered with event posters that say *Universités de Paris*. It's not a glamorous old edifice with arches and columns, like others on campus, but slab concrete.

I climb stairs to a second floor office and knock on a door that says: PÉNÉLOPE CONSTANT, DIRECTRICE DES ÉTUDES INTERNATIONALES.

"Entrez!" A woman's voice intones from behind the door.

I step in. The office looks cozier inside than out. And its tenant is a vivacious woman in her thirties with an engaging smile. We exchange *Bonjours* and she invites me to sit across from her. The pleasant floral notes of her perfume reach me even before I plant myself in my chair.

"Kai," Pénélope says in barely accented English, "how may I assist you?"

"I'm trying to deliver an envelope to a former Paradise College student who's been keeping company with one Pierre Garneaux. Pierre apparently claims to be a graduate of the Sorbonne. Could you verify if he was ever enrolled? And if he graduated?"

"It's not an uncommon name," Pénélope replies. "And technically all information in student records is private and confidential."

"I understand," I say, hoping she'll bend the rules.

"But since you have been sent by a bona fide faculty member, I could give you the most basic information."

"Thanks so much."

Her fingers dance on her computer keyboard and she gazes at her screen. "Is Pierre's family from Lyon?"

"I believe his family is from Lyon, now that you mention it."

"*Voilà!* Pierre Garneaux graduated with a degree in philosophy one year ago. You did not ask but I can tell you that he won an award for academic excellence. It appears he was a fine and serious student."

"Really?" I say. "He's since then taken up painting. That's all he seems to do. And he has two lovely young women in his life who model for him. And so on."

"Well, then, he is a lucky Pierre, isn't he?"

"Yes, I suppose he is lucky."

"Now I remember something else about Pierre," she says. "It's public knowledge, so there is no breach in confidentiality in passing it along."

"What?" I ask.

"Not exactly about Pierre. I believe he's the Pierre Garneaux whose father was sued over a fatal traffic accident in Lyon. The news of the suit traveled all the way to Paris."

"*Hmmm.* I don't know what this could have to do with Marie, but I appreciate your sharing it with me."

"Is there anything else?" Pénélope asks.

"No. You've been helpful. Thank you so much—uh, *Merci!*"

"You're welcome. Please tell Vivienne I hope she's doing better. What a terrible thing she's going through during her term in Paris. *Terrible.*"

"Yes, terrible." I say, wondering what Pénélope is talking about. Maybe Vivienne's tears at the *Sacré Coeur?*

I trot out my best *"Au revoir"* and make my way down the stairs, considering the new information Pénélope Constant has given me. Pierre was hardly a hanger-on at the Sorbonne. He was not only a graduate, but an honored graduate.

Why is the emerging picture of Pierre so at odds with the doctor's view of him?

twelve

It's midafternoon when I hike the nippy streets back to Ryan's room. After I thaw by the radiator, I pull out my laptop and make some case notes. Then I let myself catch up on sleep in the hanged man's bed.

I'm woken by my phone's alarm in time to leave for dinner. I slip on my jacket and head back out into the cold. I trek the few short blocks to Boulevard Saint-Germain and then pace by the early evening glow of stylish shops and eateries along the wide sidewalks.

The lengthy blocks of the boulevard gradually pass by. I look behind me every so often. No Citroën. Is it because I'm without Vivienne?

On the last corner of Boulevard Saint-Germain I step into Chez René. I don't see Vivienne, but I manage to communicate with the maître d'. He leads me to a table for two.

While waiting for her I take in the ambience. Chez René is a cozy French bistro with white tablecloths, mosaic tile floor, and windows overlooking the boulevard. Picassos and other reprints of masterpieces hang on the walls. About half of the three-dozen small tables are already occupied. Waiters scurry from table to table. One waiter passing by leaves two menus with me just as Vivienne appears.

"Sorry I'm a little late," she says, her lovely voice reason enough to forgive her. "I had to find my Metro map to show you the trains to Rue Saint-Dominique."

I push the table back and she slides into the red leather banquette against the wall. I return to the wooden chair opposite her. In her little black dress she looks as chic as any woman in the restaurant, French or otherwise.

The waiter returns with a sliced baguette and asks in passable English if we'd like wine. Vivienne answers in French. The one word I understand is *Bordeaux*. I consider asking how her appointment went this afternoon, but don't. Did it concern the terrible thing Pénélope mentioned? If Vivienne wants to tell me, she will.

Meanwhile she scans the menu and explains that Chez René is renowned for bistro classics like *Coq Au Vin*, *Boeuf Bourguignon*, and *Confit de Canard*. She translates: chicken or beef slow simmered in red wine and preserved duck poached in its rendered fat.

The waiter returns with the bottle of Bordeaux, removes the cork, and pours the ruby wine. I pick up my glass and inhale the smoky aroma.

Vivienne proposes a toast. "May you deliver your envelope tomorrow. And then have a little fun."

We sip. The wine tastes of wild berries, but deeper and more complex. It loosens my tongue.

"Funny thing," I say, "our resident psychic above the *lei* shop predicted I'd take a trip to a foreign country. I didn't believe her. Then I got the call from Serena. And here I am."

"We never know," Vivienne says. "Maybe I should have your psychic look into my future?"

"Careful, you could end up like me on an unexpected journey."

"I may be ready for that," she replies. Before she can elaborate the waiter returns and takes our dinner orders.

My cell phone chimes.

"Excuse me." I glance at my phone. "It's Dr. Grimes."

"Go ahead," she says. "That's why you're here."

The text says, "Glad you are making progress. Why do you think you're being followed? I have no clue."

I relay the message to Vivienne, since there's nothing in it she shouldn't know.

"Do you believe him?" she asks.

"He's my client." I shrug.

"Still I wonder why he's so insistent about contacting Marie. And what's inside that envelope."

"I assume it's a warning about the evils of Pierre and the evils of Paris. And the doctor no doubt encourages her to come home."

"That makes as much sense as anything," she replies. "But to go to such lengths to deliver a message—to have it hand-carried all the way from Honolulu. That's extreme."

The waiter returns with our main courses and pours more wine. My *Beef Bourguignon* resembles beef stew, but slow cooking in red wine brings out layers of flavor like I've never tasted before—and may never taste again. Vivienne's *Coq Au Vin* looks and smells equally divine. She takes a bite and then starts talking about her husband.

"I met Jeremy while I was on that fellowship in Brussels," she explains. "He was a fellow too. When a last-minute position opened up at Paradise College, he applied and was hired. He flew back to Hawai'i with me. That's why I didn't answer your emails. I'm sorry."

"You're married and you're happy," I say. "No need to be sorry."

She takes another bite and says nothing. The meal continues pleasantly enough through dessert, but with more silences from Vivienne.

Stepping outside after dinner into the lights of Saint-Germain we can see our breath. We walk briskly to Vivienne's apartment near the top of a quiet street called Rue du Cardinal Lemoine. She opens a courtyard gate to an array of small flats and unlocks the door to her own.

The glowing warmth inside is inviting, but I say goodnight and turn back into the cold.

She calls after me, "Kai, may I tell you something?"

I face her again. "Sure."

More tears.

"What's wrong, Viv?"

"I—" She pauses, her voice husky again.

I step into her flat. She reaches for me but when I come close her arms drop.

"I'm sorry, Kai," she whispers. "I thought I was ready, but I guess not."

"You can tell me, Viv. I'm listening."

"Let's save it until tomorrow." She wipes away a tear. "Why don't you come for breakfast? About nine? Then we can go over that Metro map. Sorry I forgot at dinner."

"No worries," I reply. "Are you sure you're okay?"

She waits for a moment, as if she's checking her pulse. "Yes, I'm okay."

I step back into the cold and tramp through the darkened streets of the Latin Quarter, mulling over what Vivienne wants to tell me.

thirteen

The next morning, Saturday, April 6, I awake a little before eight and check my phone. Nothing from Dr. Grimes. Then I remember I neglected to answer his text from late last night.

Since it's now early evening in Honolulu, I respond: "No question we are being followed by two men in a grey Citroën. The car turned up in both locations of our search. Will let you know any further developments."

I don't tell Dr. Grimes where I'm going today. And I don't tell him I'm going solo, without Vivienne. If he's knows anything about the two men tailing me, I certainly don't want to give him, and them, today's itinerary. Then I consider again the outside chance that the Citroën has nothing to do with Dr. Grimes or his stepdaughter, but with Vivienne and the terrible thing Pénélope mentioned.

But the doctor stays on my mind. I take a few minutes to search his name on my laptop, since I had no time to do it before leaving Honolulu. It turns out Dr. Grimes has practiced in Honolulu for eighteen years without a blemish on his record. Except one. And now I recall why his name looked familiar to me on Serena's note. Just last year a female patient accused him of sexual assault. And she claimed she wasn't his only victim. Dr. Grimes vehemently denied the allegation. I find a flurry of archived stories from the local newspaper. And then nothing. This could mean her allegation was dropped or she settled out of court.

After I shower and dress, I put the envelope in my pocket and walk to Vivienne's apartment. This morning the Paris skyline is cloudless blue. The air is still cool, but the sun is slowly climbing over the Seine. I walk on the sunny side of Place du Panthéon and soak up the rays. It almost feels like spring.

Vivienne is in better spirits this morning. She's in slacks and sweater, prepared to lead her student excursion to Versailles. She doesn't mention last night or what she wanted to talk about. Again, I figure she'll tell me when she's ready.

We step into her kitchenette to a small table arrayed with croissants, fresh melon, and coffee. I help myself.

"How's the jetlag this morning?' she asks.

"Better. How'd you sleep?"

"So-so. After you left Jeremy called and we talked for nearly an hour. Very late for me. Not so late for him. He's in Princeton, you know."

"Yes, you mentioned." I'm not surprised I don't like hearing her husband's name. "Are you rested enough to lead your excursion today?"

"I'll manage. You're sure you don't want to come along to Versailles? The palace and the grounds are magnificent."

"Love to," I say, "but I've got this envelope to deliver."

Vivienne spreads a Paris Metro map on the table. "If you're not coming with me to Versailles, I'd better show you how to get to Rue Saint-Dominique." She goes over the Metro route from Maubert-Mutualité. On three different trains.

"You might get on the wrong train." She looks worried. "And end up who knows where."

"I can always take a taxi."

She brightens. "That's a splendid idea."

Then I reconsider. "But I don't like sitting in traffic and watching the meter run," I say. "It's not about the money. I've got plenty of euros."

She gives me a look.

"What if I just walk along the Seine to the Eiffel Tower?" I run my finger along the river on the map. "No way I'd get lost."

"You can do that, but it's more than two miles, I'd say."

"I don't mind walking," I reply. "And I'll see some of the city that way."

"Okay, I'll write out a few phrases you can use to inquire about Marie."

Vivienne does and goes over them with me.

"Thanks," I say, taking the phrases from her. "One last favor," I say. "The woman you spoke with in Montmartre said Marie and Pierre moved to Rue Saint-Dominique above the restaurant of a popular new chef. Do you know that chef?"

"Let me see." Vivienne searches on her tablet for restaurants on Rue Saint-Dominique. It doesn't take her long. "Everybody in Paris knows that chef," she says. "Christian Dubois-Renard."

"And the name of his restaurant?"

"*Hmmm.* He has more than one." Vivienne searches again. "Actually, he has three: Café Christian, Les Pâtés, and Chez Renard. All on that same street."

"Is that unusual? For a chef to have three restaurants on the same street?"

"It's not unusual for a popular chef to have more than one restaurant, but not necessarily all on the same street." She gives me the addresses, we agree to meet for dinner at a famous Left Bank café, and I'm on my way.

The sooner I deliver that envelope to Marie, the sooner I can concentrate on the puzzle of Vivienne.

fourteen

I consult my Paris map and start walking down Rue du Cardinal Lemoine. After about a block I take Rue Monge toward the river. Despite the continuing cool, sidewalk cafés are already in full swing. Blue sky and full sun have coaxed patrons out at this early hour on a Saturday morning. They sit in the glow of gas heaters sipping hot-spiced wine, coffee, and chocolate. The atmosphere is festive.

Me, I'm taking a hike. I console myself that at least I'm seeing a bit of Paris. And what better way than on foot?

I cross Boulevard Saint-Germain and soon I'm walking in a westerly direction along the Seine, the sun warming my back. Bookstalls along the riverbank display their colorful wares—including tiny replicas of the Eiffel Tower. I can't see the real tower myself yet. I consult my map again to verify I'm on the right track. Then I scan cars whizzing along the river quayside. No grey Citroën. Yet.

But there's plenty else to see: glass-topped excursion boats chugging up the river, the soaring spires of the Cathedral of Notre Dame, and the magnificent Louvre museum. Vivienne has thoughtfully circled these and other sites on the map.

Déjà vu. Paradise College's promo video: *That's you atop the Eiffel Tower! That's you admiring the Mona Lisa at the Louvre!*

Not quite. I start a mental list of Top Ten Paris Attractions I'm not likely to visit.

My phone chimes. It's Dr. Grimes again: "Please update me on your search."

I step away from the pedestrian traffic and reply: "Heading to another location in Paris with the envelope. Reason to believe Marie is there. Will report back when I have news."

Again, I don't tell him where I'm going.

I continue walking. When the river winding through the center of Paris bends sharply left I finally see it, rising surreal above the ornate old buildings. Another of those Top Ten Paris Attractions: The Eiffel Tower.

Only a block or so from the tower I pick up Rue Saint-Dominique, a narrow canyon-like Left Bank street of sidewalk-level shops and residences above them. The street's main draw seems to be the famous tower hovering over it. After passing a few shops I notice something that stops me. Among the cars, mopeds, and vans parked along the street is the grey Citroën. Same two men inside.

I feel again for the envelope in my pocket and ask myself once more the obvious question: Why are these two men following me?

Having already rehearsed multiple answers to the question, I just keep walking. Well, I do note the absence of Vivienne, yet the continued presence of the Citroën. That may rule her out. But it may not. And my leaving Dr. Grimes in the dark about the location of my search today doesn't remove him either. Unless the Citroën has nothing to do with either of them. Or with the envelope.

The first restaurant operated by the famous chef I come to is a rustic corner eatery whose wraparound awning says *Café Christian*.

I step in. The place is hopping. At a dozen small tables diners are enjoying glistening duck legs, wine-glazed chicken breasts, and green salads with goat's cheese and grilled bread. *Bon appétit!*

A waiter hails me, *"Bonjour. Une table pour un?"*

I pull out Marie's photo and try the French phrase *"Connaissez-vous cette femme?"* that Vivienne said means, "Do you know this woman?"

Surprisingly, the waiter seems to understand. He studies the photo. "No, I don't know her," he replies in English.

"Her father is looking for her," I say, hoping that will motivate him to cooperate. "She may be living with this man on Rue Saint-Dominique." I pull out the photo of Pierre.

"I do not know him either. But let me ask our maître d'." He takes both photos and disappears up some stairs.

While waiting I scan the restaurant. The walls, as at the Saint-Germain bistro Chez René, are lined with paintings. The waiter returns with the maître d', who says he hasn't seen Marie but he has seen Pierre.

"Recently?" I ask.

"Yes, a few days ago. He brought two paintings for display."

"Do you know where he lives?"

"No, but with the paintings there may be an address."

"May I see them?"

"Oui," responds maître d'.

I follow him upstairs to another small dining room with a dozen more tables. Floor to ceiling windows overlooking

Rue Saint-Dominique are shut today against the cool air. On the walls hang more paintings. The maître d' leads me to two side-by-side that look identical. But on closer inspection I can see that one on the left has a provocative twist.

"Do you know Renoir's *Jeunes filles au piano*—young girls at the piano?" He points to the painting on the right.

"Not really," I say. But the painting does look vaguely familiar: two teenage girls in satin dresses—a blonde seated at an upright piano and a brunette standing close beside her—both gaze at a score on the music stand. It appears to be a moment of closeness between them. The flush of their cheeks echoes the luminous pink folds of the curtain behind them. The colors are beautifully-modulated pastels, glowing with life.

"Pierre has paid homage to Renoir," the maître d' points to the painting on the left, "while cleverly changing the subjects to his own two sisters."

His *sisters?* When I look closely at the girls' faces in Pierre's version I see—unmistakably—the visages of Marie and the woman apparently called Nicole. Marie, with her golden brown hair, sits on the piano bench; the darker-featured Nicole, looking a few years older, stands beside her. Same poses as in the Renoir painting. But instead of girls—beautiful young women.

I have to admit that Pierre has nailed Renoir's glowing hues, at least to my untrained eye. I can see why Vivienne said the young artist shows promise.

From the homage painting hangs a tag on a string that says—*Jeunes filles au piano revisité*—Pierre LeTrois—1,200 €. On the reverse side is his web and email addresses. That's it.

I take a photo of the tag, both sides, with my phone. And of the LeTrois painting.

"Try down the street at the Les Pâtés and next door at Chez Renard. I believe they are displaying Pierre's paintings there too. Someone in either restaurant may know where he lives."

I say, *"Merci,"* and walk down about half a block to the second restaurant on Rue Saint-Dominique operated by chef Christian Dubois-Renard. Over my shoulder I see the Citroën still parked across the street. Only one man, this time, inside. I look directly behind me and see the other stepping into Café Christian. He's in my footsteps again. And making more inquiries about what?

Les Pâtés has the same casual ambience of Café Christian, but the décor of this second restaurant resembles an American diner. A counter with a dozen chrome swivel stools and a foot rail runs nearly the entire length of the establishment. Only one or two customers—by now it's after the lunch hour— hunch over little iron pots with what look like casseroles and stews inside, smelling like a Hawai'i plate lunch gone to heaven. As in the chef's other restaurant, along the walls hang prints of masterpieces.

A waiter strides up to me and utters a blur of French.

I respond, *"Parlez-vous anglais?"*

"A little," he says, hesitantly. And then, "I am very sorry, *monsieur,* we are closing. We serve again at the five o'clock hour."

I pull out Marie's photo and ask: "Have you seen her?"

He pauses for a moment and then replies, *"Non, monsieur."*

"Have you seen him?" I show him Pierre's photo.

He lights up. *"Oui, monsieur."*

Now we're getting somewhere.

"Allons-y," he says.

He leads me to the back of the restaurant. In a dim corner hang two nearly identical paintings again—a masterpiece and an homage copy. This time the masterpiece is not French but, appropriate to this diner, American. It's a rural, agricultural scene. A bald grim old farmer stands holding up a pitchfork, with a much younger woman standing grimly by his side. I remember the name of the painting: "American Gothic." But I couldn't tell you the artist's name.

The waiter has it on the tip of his tongue: Grant Wood.

Next to the Grant Wood is a version by Pierre LeTrois. The artist himself becomes the old farmer with the pitchfork and in the frame with him is not one young woman, but two, on either side. Marie and Nicole. Their expressions are not dour as in the original, but smiling and playful. The mood is lighthearted. A tag hangs from the frame—*American Gothic Revisité*—1,500 €.

The Grant Wood could hardly be further in technique from the Renoir, but again Pierre appears to have nailed it. I assume the restaurant gets a cut of the sale. So someone here must know where the artist lives. I ask if the waiter and wonder if he too will wander off to find a maître 'd'.

The waiter stays put and says *"Non, monsieur."*

"You have no idea?" I say in English.

He surprises me by responding, "Why do you not try next door at Chez Renard? Our chef knows Pierre's father, a wine merchant. Chef Christian is watching over the young man."

"Why—watching over him?"

"You would have to ask our chef, *monsieur.*" The waiter heads for the house phone. "I will call. But I can promise you nothing."

I march next door to Chez Renard.

fifteen

It's all starting to make some kind of wacky sense. Pierre can display his clever homage paintings in Christian Dubois-Renard's three restaurants because the young artist's father, a wine merchant, knows the chef.

Chez Renard appears to be the chef's flagship restaurant. Potted cypress trees flank the glass and polished brass entry doors, creating the impression of elegance.

I try the doors. Locked. The posted hours of operation indicate that this is a dinner establishment. But the staff inside are already scurrying. I knock and one head inside turns. It's a young man carefully arranging wine glasses. He approaches the door and opens it just a crack.

"*Bonjour*," I say. "The chef is expecting me."

The young man looks surprised. I haul out my photo of Pierre and try to convey that the staff at Les Pâtés sent me to inquire about him.

"Come with me." He opens the door.

Inside fine porcelain, crystal, and silver grace white tablecloths. Masterpieces hang on the walls. As we walk through the elegant dining room I check out the paintings for evidence of Pierre. I see no Marie. No Nicole. But I do see LeTrois himself in a strange homage to Van Gogh.

It's that self-portrait in which the artist sports a bandage over his right ear. I vaguely remember the story about his ear, but am not sure it's a true story: Van Gogh severed the ear in a fit of lunacy and presented it to a woman, just as a matador traditionally presents a bull's ear to a special lady.

In Pierre's version the young French artist himself has assumed the same pose and is wearing an identical bandage over his ear. Though LeTrois looks nothing like Van Gogh, Pierre manages to reproduce the legendary artist's unique brush strokes. But unlike LeTrois's other two copies, this one lacks humor. This one is dark. Is there is a somber side to the playful Pierre?

The waiter leads me into a crowded kitchen of gleaming stainless steel. Prep chefs are busily dicing vegetables, slicing duck legs and chicken breasts and fish filets and beef tenderloins, and arranging salads, side dishes, and desserts. The food is beautiful. No kidding.

Managing the prep chefs is a distinguished looking man of medium height with a full head of raven hair. His starched white double-breasted chef's jacket says: *Christian Dubois-Renard, Chef.*

The great man himself!

When the waiter shows him my photo of Pierre, the chef looks instantly suspicious.

"Que voulez-vous avec Pierre?" he says. The waiter translates, "What do you want with Pierre?"

"Tell the chef I don't want anything with Pierre," I reply. "I'm looking for his American girlfriend." I show him her photo. "Her stepfather sent me from Hawai'i to deliver an envelope to her."

The waiter translates and then the chef, looking more curious now than suspicious, says through the waiter:"Pierre's father is worried about him and his sister too."

There's that sister reference again. I ask: "Why is Pierre's father worried?"

The chef cannot tell me.

"I know Pierre is living on Rue Saint-Dominique," I say. "Do you know where?"

The waiter explains that the chef is sworn to secrecy by Pierre's father.

The chef himself is starting to look impatient, if not agitated. Plus he's standing next to a wood block containing a dozen large carving knives. I take the hint.

"Merci," I say. "You've been very helpful.

The waiter leads me back to the glass front doors and I try one last time to find out where Pierre lives.

He replies: "I cannot tell you without risking my job, *monsieur*. But—how do you say in English?—you are very warm."

"Merci." I step back onto the sidewalk of Rue Saint-Dominique and gaze up at the apartments above the res-taurant. *Voilà!*

Next to Chez Renard is a door leading to those apartments. Inside the doorway I find rows of buttons with apartment numbers next to them. There must be four dozen buttons, most with names of the occupants next to them. Scanning the names, I don't see Marie Ho or Pierre Garneaux or Pierre LeTrois. But there is one button—4J—with a name beside it that attracts my attention. Nicole. No last name.

I push button 4J.

The intercom rings and I wait.

A woman answers—*"Allô!"*—sounding very French.

"Parlez-vous anglais?" I ask.

She says, "Yes, a little. "

"Is Marie there?"

"No," The woman says. "There is no person here by that name."

"How about Pierre Garneaux? Or Pierre LeTrois."

"Au revoir." She abruptly hangs up.

Her abruptness, if not her rudeness, suggests that I've hit gold. If I'm right, all I have to do now is somehow encounter Marie and put the envelope in her hands. I decide to post myself where I can watch the building's entrance.

Just beyond Chez Renard on the same side of the street is a little *crêperie.* Though most restaurants seem to be closed during the lull between lunch and dinner, this one is open and has a few tables on the sidewalk that would offer a good vantage point.

I sit at one of the tables. It's cool for outdoor dining and I'm the only one out here. Before long a woman brings me a menu in French. I may be here for a while, so I point to *crêpe poulet.* The word *poulet* I recognize from my phrasebook as chicken. Seems safe.

She retreats. I pull the envelope from my pocket and set it on the table. Across the street, down about a half block, the Citroën sits in the loading zone. The second man is back inside with the driver now.

A blue-light police cruiser pulls alongside the Citroën. The officer gets out, speaks to the driver, and then makes a sweeping gesture like he's telling him to move on. The Citroën pulls away from the curb and passes by the *crêperie.* The man in the passenger seat glares at me as the car goes by.

I wait for my crepe and keep an eye on both sides of the street. I'm not concerned Marie or Pierre will spot me and shy away. Neither knows what I look like. To them I would be just another tourist on the sidewalks of Paris.

The Citroën passes by again and stops on the other side of the street. The passenger steps out on the sidewalk. He leans against a light pole. I put the envelope back into my pocket. It appears he's going to hang out there as long as I sit at this *crêperie*.

My crepe arrives. It's a large and thin and delicate pancake filled with diced chicken in a rich cream sauce. *Delicious.* I wish I had ordered two. I watch the man across the street as I work on the crepe. He's on his cell phone now. The woman eventually returns and I pay her and ask if she minds if I sit a while longer. I'm not sure she understands me, but she looks at the empty tables and shrugs.

People stroll by on the sidewalk. Time passes.

Then a young couple walking arm-in-arm toward the *crêperie* catches my eye. They are chatting and smiling and stepping lively. The woman is smoking.

It's Marie. Her companion is Pierre.

Marie is the diminutive and spritely island girl I expected. And Pierre is the tall young Frenchman.

Marie takes a casual puff from her cigarette as they approach. Up close I can see both brightness and sadness in her eyes.

The man across the street puts away his phone. He's watching Marie and Pierre as closely as I am. That doesn't stop me. This may be my one and only chance. I rise as the couple reaches the *crêperie* and I step toward them.

"Marie," I say, "this is for you." I hand her the envelope.

She takes it, sees her name, and her face pales. "What is this?" She sounds suspicious, frightened.

"I don't know what's inside," I respond. "I was just asked to deliver it to you."

She eyes me warily.

"Allez, Pierre," she says to her boyfriend. *"Allons-y!"*

They rush away.

sixteen

Marie and Pierre disappear with the envelope into the doorway next to Chez Renard.

I'm a little let down. I don't know what I expected. A smile? A hug?

C'mon. I purposely didn't introduce myself. I was a stranger to them. Frankly, I'm surprised Marie even took the envelope. Well, it did have her name on it. Main thing, my job is done.

I glance at my phone. It's after five in Paris, which means very early morning in Honolulu. Dr. Grimes will most likely be asleep. But he told me to let him know immediately.

I text the doctor: "Delivered envelope to Marie."

I walk back toward the Eiffel Tower, glancing again at the Citroën parked on Rue Saint-Dominique. Both men are inside now, talking on their phones. They appear too busy to pay attention to me. In fact, I think I've ceased to interest them. I head to the quayside boulevard fronting the tower where taxis line the curb. I have neither the time nor the inclination to hike back to the Latin Quarter.

Before stepping into a taxi I purchase from a street vendor a postcard of the Eiffel Tower for Shirley, a.k.a. Madame Zenobia, resident psychic at Fujiyama's Flower Leis. I imagine myself handing it to her and saying, "Here's your postcard from nowhere"—my way of admitting Madame's crystal ball was right. More likely, she took a wild stab and got lucky. I take wild stabs sometimes myself. But I rarely get so lucky.

I tell the taxi driver, "44 Rue des Écoles." We take off in a flash. After getting caught in late afternoon traffic, I'm back in Ryan's room at a little before six. I shower, dress, and then hoof it down Boulevard Saint-Germain to the famous Parisian café where I'm to meet Vivienne.

Les Deux Magots sits on the corner of Place Saint-Germain-des-Prés, named apparently for the beautiful old church opposite the café. In warmer weather the wicker tables and chairs under the café's green awning would no doubt sit in the open air, but tonight sliding glass doors enclose them against the twilight chill.

When I step inside the maître d' confirms he has a reservation for two under the name Vivienne—not Stone but the more French-sounding Duvane. Maybe she gets better service using her maiden name?

The maître d' leads me to one of a half dozen small tables along a banquette. The tables are close together by American standards. You could brush shoulders with nearby diners. Every culture, I guess, has its version of personal space. For now, I sit alone in a chair opposite the banquette, saving the more comfortable leather for Vivienne.

Scanning the café I spot two clay men in traditional Chinese garb seated near the ceiling in chairs affixed to a large pillar— the *deux magots* or figurines from the Far East that Vivienne told me about at breakfast. The two gaze serenely over the dining room. I would say they are also chatting, except they're sitting on different sides of the pillar, facing away from each other.

"Studying the *deux magots*?" Vivienne sneaks up on me.

I rise and we hug politely. She sits in the banquette across from me looking grand, as usual. Being drawn to her feels as natural as breathing.

"So tell me about your day," she says. "Did you deliver the envelope to Marie?"

"I did."

Before she can respond the waiter shows up.

Then Vivienne says, "Let's celebrate with champagne, shall we, Kai?"

"Absolutely," I reply.

She tells the waiter: *"Une bouteille de Champagne de la maison, s'il vous plaît."*

"Merci," he responds and departs.

"How was Versailles?" I ask her.

"Busy on a Saturday, as expected. But my students' eyes were wide as saucers. I don't think the crowds mattered compared to the grandeur of the place."

"Sorry I missed it."

"Tomorrow is Sunday. How about I show you around Paris? We could do all the touristy things: stroll the Champs-Elysées, climb the Arc de Triomphe. Whatever you like."

"You're on. I may never get back here again."

"So tell me about Marie," Vivienne says. "Where did you find her?"

I launch into a shortened version of my walking along the Seine, visiting three of the renowned chef's restaurants, and ultimately handing Marie the envelope near one of them.

"And the Citroën," she asks. "Did it follow you again?"

"Yes, with both men aboard."

"Strange," she replies.

The waiter returns with the champagne and a silver bucket filled with ice. He eases the cork from the bottle with a muted pop and pours a taste for Vivienne. She holds her glass up to the light and peers into the rising bubbles. Then she takes in its aroma and sips.

"Magnifique," she tells the waiter. *"Merci beaucoup."*

"Voilà!" He fills our two glasses, puts the champagne bottle in the silver bucket, and departs.

"Here's to you, Kai." She raises her glass. "You did it."

"And to you, Vivienne. Couldn't have done it without you."

"I doubt that," she says. "But I have something to celebrate too. It's not a great accomplishment like yours—more of a failure, really. A painful but necessary step forward in my life."

"Let's toast it." I raise my glass and wonder if she's referring to that *terrible thing.*

Vivienne hoists her glass, lowers her pitch, and says, "To my divorce."

My expression changes.

Vivienne notices. "You're the first to know."

I look at her left hand. The rock is gone. "So that's why you made the reservation tonight under the name Duvane? And why you were crying at the *Sacré Coeur?*"

She nods. "And why I had that appointment yesterday—a conference call with Jeremy and our attorneys."

I hold back a smile. "Here's to your being single again."

We drink.

Then Vivienne explains: "The divorce isn't my idea. When Jeremy took the job at Princeton and we started living apart, he became very close to another professor there. Jeremy didn't say so, but I think he met Bill earlier at a conference. Anyway, a few months ago he told me he and Bill were in love."

"So Jeremy's gay?"

"He's a sweet guy and would never intentionally hurt me, but I'm sure Jeremy loves that man more than he ever loved me."

"That's no knock on you," I say. "Sounds like Jeremy didn't know himself very well when he married you."

"No, he didn't." Her voice quiets almost to a whisper. "But, still, it hurts. Losing a husband to another woman is one thing. But losing a husband to a man?"

"You're plenty woman for any man who likes women," I say, the bubbly loosening my tongue.

She manages a smile. "Thanks, Kai. Reassurance helps. It really does."

We both sip and she continues. "Jeremy is not making the divorce any harder than it has to be. He's giving me our home in Kailua. And I'm letting him keep our beautiful retriever, Sadie, who's been with him while I'm in Paris. Very sad."

"No reason why you couldn't visit Sadie in Princeton," I say. "Since you and Jeremy are still on good terms."

"Except that I don't want to see him with his lover."

I could invite Vivienne when she returns to Hawai'i to hang out with my retriever, Kula. But that would involve explaining about Kula's foster mom. Even though the pet detective and I are no longer dating, I hold off.

The waiter returns, we order, and then drink champagne until he comes back with our food.

"Bon appétit," Vivienne says.

Between bites she wants to know about the connection between Chef Christian Dubois-Renard and young Pierre Garneaux, a.k.a. Pierre LeTrois. I explain that the chef knows Pierre's father, a wine merchant in Lyon, who is concerned about his son. And that appears to be the whole point of Pierre and Marie moving to Rue Saint-Dominique above his flagship restaurant.

"Did the chef say why Pierre's father was concerned?" Vivienne asks.

"No, but the Citroën suggests somebody has an interest in Pierre or Marie or maybe in the other woman."

"Could that somebody be Marie's own stepfather?"

"It could," I respond. "But why would he hire me and the Citroën too?"

"To check up on you? To make sure you delivered the envelope?"

"Or to take over after I delivered it?"

"Take over for what?" she asks.

"I might be able to answer that if I knew what was inside that envelope."

My phone chimes. A text from Dr. Grimes. I glance at it first and then read aloud: "Brilliant, Kai! One last request: Marie's address, if you have it. Many thanks, GJG."

"Are you going to give it to him?" Vivienne looks concerned. "Since Marie herself was apparently unwilling."

"If the doctor hired the Citroën, he already knows where Marie lives. I would only be confirming. In any case, I'll be vague."

I text back: "Located Marie on a side street near Eiffel Tower. Mahalo, Kai."

"You think that will do it?"

"It will have to," I say, emboldened by the champagne. "The problem in Paris is over."

After dinner I walk Vivienne to her apartment. Despite the evening chill, the bubbly has put both of us in a warm and mellow mood.

Vivienne invites me in for a nightcap. She pours cognac and we sit across from each other in her cozy apartment, just inches apart. We reminisce. I reach for her hand. It's been years since our whirlwind week together in Honolulu, but we slip back easily into the groove.

Then she suddenly withdraws her hand.

"What's wrong?" I ask her.

"I'm sorry, Kai," she says. "It's not you. It's me. I need a little more time. I know my marriage is over, but I'm not quite over it yet."

"No hurry." I try not to sound disappointed. "Maybe another time?" I say, forever hopeful.

After our cognacs and a long goodbye, plus another invitation to breakfast, I weave my way back toward Rue des Écoles. It's after midnight and not getting any warmer. My breath puffs white clouds under the streetlamps. It starts to rain. My thin jacket is a joke. I wander alone and shivering in the dim and drizzly streets of the Latin Quarter.

I get lost in the deluge and find myself on a deserted lane called Rue d'Ulm. Suddenly I'm standing in front of a dark and shuttered eatery called Café Waikīkī. I rub my eyes. Yes, that's the name of the place.

Waikīkī. The surf lesson. Vivienne Duvane. If it's an omen, why am I out in the cold instead of in her warm apartment?

I start moving again. I'm not exactly stumbling, but I'm not exactly walking straight either. I notice a car coming up behind me. The Citroën?

The car pulls up beside me.

Not the Citroën. A police cruiser. An officer rolls down his passenger-side window part way.

"Bonsoir, Monsieur," he says. *"Puis-je vous aider?"*

I give my standard response: *"Parlez-vous anglais?"*

And he gives his expected, "Yes, a little."

"I'm just walking home," I say, "to Rue des Écoles."

How much the officer understands I'm not sure. But he motions me, cordially enough, to move along. He seems to be waiting for me to start walking again. But then the radio inside the car crackles and there's a barrage of French. The only words I understand are "Rue Saint-Dominique."

The officer rolls up his window, turns on his siren, and roars away on the wet pavement. I somehow find my way, drenched and shivering, back to the hanged man's bed.

seventeen

The next morning, Sunday, April 7, Vivienne and I sit across from each other at her breakfast table. Sunlight streams in. A television news program babbles happily in the background. The aroma of French roast coffee fills the air. We don't discuss last night. Or tonight. We talk about today: sightseeing in Paris.

We're sipping our java when something I hear on the TV news catches my attention. The name of the street where I spent most of yesterday: Rue Saint-Dominique. The same street name I heard last night from the police cruiser's radio. It's too much of a coincidence.

"What are they saying?" I ask Vivienne. She turns up the volume. Images from Rue Saint-Dominique, Eiffel Tower looming above it, fill the screen.

"A pedestrian accident, late last night." Vivienne pauses. "Hit and run."

"Do they give a name?" I have a sinking feeling.

Now we're both peering at the TV. A photo of the deceased appears. It's a familiar young Frenchman in his early twenties. The name under the photo is PIERRE GARNEAUX.

No words come to me, but Vivienne says, *"Oh, no."*

More images from Rue Saint-Dominique fill the screen—the apartment above Chez Renard where Pierre lived, the restaurant, and the famous chef himself. Then a phone number for the Paris Police. I ask Vivienne to call in the Citroën's plate. She pulls herself together and makes the call.

While she's talking on the phone something else is bothering me.

When she hangs up I say, "I'm going back to Rue Saint-Dominique,"

"Why?"

"Marie. She may not want to see me, but I'm going anyway."

"I'll go with you," Vivienne replies. "I'm quite sure she'll see me."

We walk to the Cardinal Lemoine station, ride a west-bound train nearly ten stops, change once, and then disembark at École Militaire, the closest station to Rue Saint-Dominique. On the way I compose a text to Dr. Grimes: "Pierre Garneaux is dead."

I don't elaborate. I want to see how he responds. Once we emerge from the metro station I send the message.

The sky this morning is sapphire blue. The air feels almost balmy. A sidewalk café just steps from the metro station called Café des Officiers bustles. It's a beautiful morning to sit and watch Parisian life stroll by. It's not such a beautiful morning to be dead.

My phone chimes. A reply already Dr. Grimes: "I am astonished. I did want Pierre away from my stepdaughter. I did not want him dead."

As Vivienne and I walk into Rue Saint-Dominique, I'm not sure what to believe. The doctor professes no knowledge of Pierre's death and admits no hand in it. Not that I expect he would. Why did he send me? Was I an unwitting spotter for his hit men? Was the envelope merely a decoy—nothing more inside than blank sheets of paper? Or was I on the fool's errand I thought I was—a trans-Pacific-trans-Atlantic carrier pigeon?

We pass Café Christian and Les Pâtés, and stop just beyond the Chef's flagship restaurant, Chez Renard. We step into the foyer of the apartment building and ring apartment 4J.

"Allô." A young woman answers the intercom, her French sounding good but, to my untrained ear, not native.

"It's Marie," Vivienne whispers to me, then asks her former student in English if she—Viv, that is—can come up.

Marie expresses surprise and then quickly says yes.

We don't bother with the small elevator that seems to be engaged on an upper floor. We take the stairs up four flights. I'm huffing by the time we reach the fourth floor and we walk down a narrow hallway to apartment 4J and knock.

The door opens not to Marie, but to the darker-featured French woman familiar from Pierre's paintings. Nicole is in black and, despite her understandably strained expression, is as attractive in person as on canvas. I doubt she got much sleep last night. Marie either. But that's hard to tell, because Marie is nowhere in sight.

Nicole invites us to sit down in the spacious by-Paris-standards apartment, where Pierre's unframed canvases lean against the walls. Vivienne and Nicole converse quietly in French. During a pause Vivienne turns to me and explains that a police investigator has just departed after interviewing both Nicole and Marie. The latter was with the young Frenchman when he was struck. Pierre and Nicole's parents—for Nicole is indeed Pierre's sister—are arriving momentarily from Lyon and she plans to return with them. Marie has been invited to Lyon as well, since the Garneauxs apparently think of her as their adopted daughter.

I've had the unfortunate experience more than once of meeting with loved ones of a person who has just died. My approach is always to express my condolences and then let the bereaved direct the conversation, if they wish to converse at all. But if the death pertains to a case and I feel compelled to ask questions, I try to proceed gently.

I look into Nicole's anguished eyes and say, "I'm very sorry about your brother."

She responds, "Thank you."

"Nicole, do you have any idea who would want to harm him?" If she's able to talk about it, I'm thinking she may mention Marie's stepfather, but Nicole surprises me.

"I just explained to the police investigator," she says matter-of-factly. "One of my father's delivery vans was involved in an accident in Lyon that killed the only son of a man named Gustave Beauchamp. A court awarded Monsieur Beauchamp financial compensation, but he was not satisfied. He hired agents in Paris to stalk Pierre. Pierre is my parents' only son. In Monsieur Beauchamp's warped mind, killing Pierre would constitute an eye for an eye. Even though his own son was killed by accident."

Nicole's story sounds like a fuller version of the one told to me by Pénélope Constant.

I ask Nicole, "Is that why you kept moving in Paris from one apartment to another? And why Chef Dubois-Renard was looking after Pierre?"

"Partly," says Nicole. We moved to Montmartre because Pierre desired to live there. But we fled when it became too difficult to protect ourselves from Monsieur Beauchamp."

"Were these agents also after you?"

"Killing me—my father's daughter, not his son—would not satisfy Monsieur Beauchamp's idea of justice. But just in case, Marie and I both took a self-defense course and learned how to fend off aggressive and abusive men."

Just then Marie herself enters the room, walks straight to the considerably taller Vivienne, and they hug. Viv pats her gently and says, "I'm so sorry."

Marie isn't crying. She's trembling.

Vivienne introduces me but I don't think Marie even hears my name. When she finally looks at me I can see a flash of recognition in her eyes.

"I'm sorry about your boyfriend," I say.

"The envelope," Marie says in a tremulous voice. "You're the one who gave me the envelope yesterday."

"Your stepfather asked me to deliver it. He said he was worried about you and unable to locate you himself."

"Him, worried about me?" Marie's voice sharpens. "He wants something. He always wants something."

Is this Marie's granite streak?

"I have no idea what's inside the envelope," I say.

"I don't either," she replies, sounding angry now. "When I recognized his handwriting I tossed the envelope in the rubbish bin."

"You might want to retrieve it. What's inside could have some bearing on Pierre's death."

"Too late." She shakes her head. "I'm quite sure it's gone."

I'm thinking, *so I fly seven thousand miles to deliver an envelope that goes promptly into the trash—unopened?*

When Vivienne explains I'm the private detective who investigated Ryan Song's hanging, Marie remembers our exchange of emails nearly a year ago and warms. My proving her jilted boyfriend didn't hang himself over her photo may have eased her feelings of guilt. I don't mention this. I'm just glad she's apparently unaware she only hears from me when one of her boyfriends dies.

Marie wonders aloud, "Why are you with my French professor?"

"Your French professor is my translator and guide. She helped me find you."

"She did?" Marie looks at Vivienne.

"Only for purposes of delivering the envelope," I say. "We kept your address confidential. We gave it to no one. And definitely not to your stepfather."

"Him again." Marie grimaces.

"Did you get a good look at the car that struck Pierre?" I ask.

"Not really," Marie replies. "It was night and the car seemed to come out of nowhere."

"Color?"

"Dark, I think."

"How about grey?"

"Could be," she says. "The car didn't stand out—just sort of blended in with the night."

"Did you see the driver? Or any passengers?"

"Afraid not. I was blinded by the headlights."

Nicole's cell phone rings. She answers, *"Allô."*

The call doesn't last long. Nicole hangs up and says, "My parents have reached the city. They are a few minutes from Rue Saint-Dominique."

"We'll be going then," Vivienne says. "But if we can do anything at all for you, please let us know."

"Kai," Marie says, "may I show you something before you leave?"

I nod, wondering what's up.

She leads me into a bedroom that I assume belonged to her and Pierre. French windows with a wrought iron balcony overlook Rue Saint-Dominique. The walls are hung with his paintings, mostly nudes. Some of Marie. Some of Nicole and some of other women. Is this what Marie wants to show me?

"Kai," she says in almost a whisper, "when are you flying back to Honolulu?"

"Soon," I say, assuming it may take a day or two to find available flights.

"May I come with you?" she asks. "I plan to return to Paris for Pierre's memorial service, of course, which Nicole assures me will take time to arrange."

"Sure," I say, but am surprised she would leave Paris of her own volition so suddenly, when her stepfather has been trying for months to pry her loose.

"If you'll trust me," she says, "I'll take care of everything. I have a great travel agent on Avenue Bosquet. She helps me anytime, even on weekends."

"Why don't I email you my reservation?" I pull it up on my phone.

She reminds me of her email address and I send her my reservation.

"I'll ask my agent to try for flights as early as tomorrow morning," Marie says. "Is that too soon?"

I consider the prospect of leaving tomorrow. That means only one night with Vivienne, if I'm lucky. I almost object. But one night is better than none. "If you can get us out of Paris tomorrow, go for it."

"We'll have plenty of time to talk on those long flights," she says.

I'm not sure what she thinks we have to talk about, but I nod.

Marie walks back to the living room and I follow. Vivienne and Nicole are still conversing quietly in French. Marie approaches them and joins the conversation. She speaks to Nicole. I hear the words Honolulu and Lyon. I assume she's explaining that she's returning with me rather than accompanying Nicole and her parents. The two women hug.

Vivienne then says "*Au revoir*" to Nicole and Marie.

"I'll be in touch about the airline tickets," Marie says to me. And then to Vivienne: "See you tonight. *Merci beaucoup.*"

On the way down the stairs, Vivienne explains that since Marie did not feel comfortable staying alone in the empty Rue Saint-Dominique apartment after Nicole's departure, Vivienne offered to share her own tiny apartment with Marie until she and I return to Honolulu. That keeps me until then in the hanged man's bed.

"I'm so sorry, Kai." Viv doesn't explain. She doesn't need to.

We both know what that means.

Our reunion will have to wait.

eighteen

After one last dinner with Vivienne, Marie in tow, I'm alone again in Ryan's room.

I can't sleep, so I size up my brief April in Paris. There was the unseasonable chill, the Top Ten Attractions I didn't visit, the promise of a rekindled love unfulfilled, and the specter of another promising young man cut down in his prime. As for Sinatra's song, there were no chestnuts in blossom, no warm embrace of spring. Only his last melancholy words about Paris in spring resonate with me now: "What have you done to my heart?"

Though the mission I was sent on, in retrospect, seems futile, I did what I was asked by Serena and by Dr. Grimes. Never mind that Marie, by her own admission, didn't see the contents of the envelope. The important thing is I delivered. Not only that, Marie is coming home to Hawai'i, which her stepfather apparently tried repeatedly to accomplish himself but failed.

What of Serena's larger purpose? Will the Ho Trust's donations continue flowing to the college? Over this, I have no control. Again, I did what I was asked.

What about Pierre Garneaux, a.k.a. Pierre LeTrois—award-winning Sorbonne graduate, promising artist and, apparently, a prince of a young man? Pierre turned out to be hardly the leech or hanger-on vilified by Marie's stepfather. Unfortunately, I may have unwittingly led Pierre's killers to him. I wonder what I could have done differently. Should I blame myself for unintended consequences? Probably not. So why can't I sleep?

Maybe because I'm leaving Paris tomorrow—for Marie's travel agent did in fact come through—without that promised night with Vivienne? Or maybe because I hear footsteps?

I searched for the young Frenchman and his girlfriend in enough Paris neighborhoods that eventually someone will identify me. I've done nothing wrong, of course. But I will get a call from Paris Police. It's just a matter of time. My returning to Honolulu won't make a bit of difference.

Last night, exuding a champagne confidence, I told Vivienne the problem in Paris was over.

Now, upon sober reflection, I'm not so sure.

Part III
Murder at Makapuʻu

The cliffs of Makapu'u soar over the southern tip of O'ahu, sheer and craggy and brooding. Visitors hike the popular Makapu'u Lighthouse Trail to see the beacon and the panoramic views of the distant islands of Moloka'i and Maui and Lana'i. But not everyone comes for the views or comes home to tell of them.

Tumbling down, bouncing off rocks and spinning like a ragdoll, a body plunges from the cliffs into the roiling surf far below. A little avalanche of pebbles and shards follows. Floating face down—lifeless—the fallen one, living and breathing only moments before, now resembles a mere speck on the deep blue sea.

one

Monday, April 8. My phone's alarm wakes me at six. Why do I have to rise this early to catch a ten o'clock flight?

I'm not in Honolulu. I'm in Paris. And I've been warned that traffic from the Left Bank to Charles de Gaulle Airport on Monday morning can be horrendous.

My last day in Paris and my only sightseeing will consist of a gridlocked expressway.

I shower, dress, pack my bag, and wait by the curb on Rue des Écoles for the taxi I ordered last night. Amber beams in the east signal the rising sun. It's almost warm—even at this hour. Not like the early April chill I've just endured. Figures, since I'm leaving today.

I gaze across the street at the gold-speared iron gates of the Collège de France, just a stone's throw from the Sorbonne. I know my way around the Latin Quarter now, after wandering lost more than once. The aroma of coffee and baking bread from the nearby *boulangerie* fills the morning air. I resist. Good thing—because the taxi pulls in front of the college at six-thirty sharp, pointed in the direction of Rue du Cardinal Lemoine where I'm to pick up Marie Ho.

When I step into street with my bag a black Mercedes screeches toward the curb and almost hits me. This happens too fast to make out the driver or the license plate. I can't tell if it's just a random careless Parisian motorist or someone trying to hit me.

The Mercedes roars away. I slink across the street, slip into the taxi, and almost ask the driver, "Did you see that?" I'm sure he did, but he probably wouldn't understand me anyway.

On the short ride to Rue du Cardinal Lemoine I try to uncoil and consider what just happened. The job I completed here only yesterday—I hesitate to call it a case—involved my flying from Honolulu to Paris at the behest of Paradise College and Marie Ho's stepfather to deliver an envelope to her. But Marie, and her boyfriend Pierre, didn't want to be found. So I walked Paris neighborhoods searching for them, all the while being followed by a grey Citroën. Not a black Mercedes.

That doesn't stop me from wondering. For when I finally found Marie and delivered the envelope, Pierre was run down that night by, I suspect, the same Citroën. The next morning Marie told me she had discarded the envelope that I carried seven-thousand miles unopened. *Hmmm.*

This is the second problem in Paris I've worked on for the college. Both involved Marie. The first concerned the death of her classmate Ryan Song found hanging over her photo. Ryan was, until Pierre, Marie's boyfriend. She has bad luck with boyfriends. They keep turning up dead in Paris.

The taxi veers right onto Rue Monge, skirts the belatedly blossoming chestnuts in Square Paul Langevin and then heads up Rue de Cardinal Lemoine. Why Marie asked to fly with me to Honolulu is unclear. She said we have a lot to talk about. I'll bring a sympathetic ear. For an heiress, she's had it rough—not just her two dead boyfriends. Her mother plunged from a cliff at Makapuʻu near where Marie's only brother perished in a surfing accident. And that was *after* her father died. Her only remaining family is her stepfather, my client Dr. Gordon Grimes. And she's not wild about him.

The taxi climbs Rue du Cardinal Lemoine and pulls to the curb in front of two familiar faces. The island girl with bobbed hair and bright sad eyes nonchalantly smoking is Marie; the willowy redhead is her former French professor and was until yesterday my Paris guide, Vivienne Stone. Uh, Vivienne *Duvane*.

Marie snuffs out her cigarette, leaves her luggage by the curb, and climbs into the taxi. To my surprise—I thought this was goodbye—Vivienne climbs in too. I'm sandwiched between them, the faint whiff of tobacco from Marie's trench coat softened by the floral scent of Vivienne's perfume. I see again the empty spot on Vivienne's ring finger. Still not used to that. Viv and I dated years ago in Honolulu before her marriage—that just ended.

"Thought I'd ride along with you to the airport," Vivienne explains. "It'll give us another hour together before the long goodbye."

"I'm in," I reply. "Not for the long goodbye, but for the hour before."

Marie turns to us with a knowing look, as if she's just discovering the secret life of her former French professor.

The driver loads Marie's luggage into the trunk with mine. I'm still a little wobbly from that near miss on Rue des Écoles, but imagine I'm masking it well.

As the taxi starts rolling Vivienne says, "Kai, you're shivering!"

"April in Paris feels like January to me," I say.

"On this balmy morning?" Vivienne shakes her head, as if to say there's no use trying to talk to a man about feelings.

Traffic leaving central Paris, it turns out, is not nearly so heavy as traffic coming in. The taxi hums along the A3 airport expressway into the climbing sun. We arrive at the Charles de Gaulle international terminal a good half hour early. I hop out and collect our bags.

And now comes the hard part. I can see the strain in Vivienne's eyes. And I feel an ache in my gut.

She whispers, "I'm ready now."

Is she finally over her ex-husband? "And I'm about to fly half way around the world," I reply

"Good things are worth waiting for," Viv says. "I'll be back in the islands in early May."

It's not a long goodbye. She hugs Marie and then hugs me. Vivienne climbs back in, eyes moist, and waves as the taxi pulls away. I wave back and pull out my handkerchief. Just in case.

The taxi disappears up the ramp to the expressway. As Marie and I wheel our bags toward the terminal, she says, "So—you and Vivienne?"

"It's complicated." I say.

Before we reach the terminal doors Marie stops. "Do you mind?" She pulls out a cigarette.

"Meet you inside," I say.

She lights up and I step in and check my phone. No messages. I guess my client, Marie's stepfather, is done with me.

I file into the back of a long line under a sign that says ECONOMY—CHECK IN. Marie catches up with me in a few minutes and says, "Not this line." She leads me to a much shorter line that says FIRST CLASS.

I give Marie a look. Her own travel agent rebooked my ticket.

"I took the liberty of having Celeste upgrade you so we can sit together and talk. I hope you don't mind."

"Mind? Are you kidding?" Then I almost say, *This must have cost you a small fortune.* But what's a small fortune to Marie Ho?

We check in, pass through expedited security, and head to the first-class lounge, which resembles a posh private club with a bountiful breakfast buffet. I get myself my last Parisian croissant and settle into a comfy chair.

When our flight to San Francisco is called, we amble down the jet-way into the spacious first-class cabin where our fellow passengers are sipping champagne and lounging in wide leather sleeper seats. Ours are in row two. Once we settle in I glance back into the economy cabin. *But for the grace of God. And of Marie Ho.*

A flight attendant asks if we'd like champagne. Marie declines. I accept. How often do I fly first class?

I sip my bubbly to the bottom. Before long my champagne flute is collected and the big Boeing taxis for what seems like a mile, roars down the runway, and climbs over the outskirts of Paris. Soon I'm looking down on the same storybook farms and villages I saw a few days ago coming in. Green pastures glow like velvet in the morning sun. A bank of clouds suddenly cuts off the view.

Marie turns to me. "Now that we're in the air we can talk."

"Okay," I reply. "Let's talk,"

"I know who ran down Pierre—and tried to run me down. I've known all along."

"Did you tell the Paris Police?"

"No. If I told them they might not let me leave. Anyway, I want to handle this myself—with your help."

"To investigate your boyfriend's death shouldn't we have stayed in Paris?"

"The man responsible is in Honolulu."

I think I know where she's going. So I say, "Pierre's sister, Nicole, has a different theory."

"I've heard her theory many times," Marie says. "She believes a Frenchman named Gustave Beauchamp hired agents in Paris to take revenge on Pierre's father by killing his only son, since Monsieur Beauchamp's only son was killed in an accident in Lyon involving one of Monsieur Garneaux's wine delivery vans. But it wasn't Beauchamp who hired those agents. Or who killed Pierre."

"How can you be so sure?" I ask.

Before she can reply we're interrupted by an announcement. It's the First Officer. We've reached cruising altitude and he invites us to sit back, relax, and enjoy the flight. I'm usually cynical about such announcements when I'm shoehorned into an economy seat, but up here in roomy first class relaxing could be a definite possibility.

Marie says, "It's not Pierre's death I want you to investigate, anyway."

I'm hoping the First Officer comes on again, because already she's losing me. Reluctantly I ask, "Then what *do* you want me to investigate?"

"My mother's death," Marie says. "She didn't fall from the cliffs at Makapu'u. She was pushed."

two

Before I can wrap my mind around that, our flight attendant brings us warm nuts and asks what we'd like to drink. Marie orders a Pinot Noir. I order a beer.

I sink my teeth into a salty cashew and ask, "You're convinced your mother didn't slip or maybe jump?"

"My mother wasn't careless and she wouldn't deliberately leave me alone in the world. It's unimaginable."

"I've heard only good things about her," I say.

"I'm prejudiced, of course, but she was a great woman. And you've no doubt heard about her giving?"

"To Paradise College, yes." I recall the underlying reason for my trip to Paris—to keep her mother's legacy flowing. "A great woman." I echo Marie

"Then there's my stepfather," she replies. "A despicable man. He's a psychiatrist, you know, and has access to all kinds of drugs. I believe he drugged my mother and drove her to Makapu'u."

"Drugs would probably show up in an autopsy," I respond. "Anyway your stepfather told me when your mother died he got nothing but the right to remain in your family home. So what would be his motive to kill her?"

"I know his motive. I told my mother something horrid about him. She found it hard to believe at first, but then she confronted him. However he answered—whether he lied or admitted it—made her decide to expose him and file for divorce. That meant my stepfather might lose his practice and maybe end up in prison."

"If he killed your mother, then why years later kill Pierre? What's the connection?"

"My stepfather wasn't trying to kill Pierre," she says. "He was trying to kill me. Why do you think he hired you to deliver that envelope?"

"I assumed to send you a message."

"No. To find me and run me down."

I try not to look skeptical. And apparently fail.

"You'll see," she says. "We have two long flights ahead of us. I will tell all."

Before she can begin our beverages arrive and there's a break in the clouds. I look out the window. A receding shoreline below suggests we're leaving France behind.

"That's the Normandy coast." Marie points. "Ahead is the English Channel. Keep watching and you'll see the white cliffs of Dover."

Across the channel I spot a cream-colored ribbon rippling along the bright blue coastline of what must be Britain. I take a good long look. It's beautiful. Once the white cliffs disappear beneath the airplane's wings I turn back to Marie. What she has to tell me, I expect, won't be so beautiful.

"One day when I was high school," she says matter-of-factly, "my stepfather came into my bedroom when my

mother was away and asked me in his creepy voice why I'd
been flirting with him. I didn't know what to say. I felt guilty.
I was a teenager, after all, and I probably was a little flirty. But
I never intended . . ."

"You don't have to tell me every detail," I say as gently as
I can. "I get the picture."

She carries on. "He said he knew why I'd been flirting.
And he was going to give me what I wanted. I'd been brought
up to respect and obey my parents. And here was this man
who was now my father, and a doctor, telling me these crazy
things. Can you imagine how confused I was?"

"I'm very sorry," I say, recalling allegations of sexual
assault by the doctor's own patients. A pattern?

"That was the first time. There were other times. Always
when my mother was away. He told me to keep it between
us. He told me I shouldn't tell anyone, especially my mother.
I felt shamed. And I thought it was my fault. So I didn't tell."

"That must have been very painful," I say, "to hold it inside
and to have nowhere to turn."

"Let me tell you what finally made him stop," Marie
continues. "Eventually I confided in an older friend. She
insisted it wasn't my fault and she encouraged me to tell my
mother. So against his orders, I did."

"And you think that's when he decided to kill her? When
your mother confronted him and asked for a divorce?"

She nods. "On the weekend my mother died he claimed
he was on Molokaʻi. And he had alibis—witnesses who saw
him there. But he could have slipped away during the night
and piloted his speedboat to Oʻahu."

"So you believe he returned to your family home, drugged
your mother, and took her to Makapuʻu?"

She nods again. "He deserves to die."

"Life in prison is the maximum sentence under Hawai'i law."

"That's not enough." Marie sips her Pinot. "Not nearly enough."

"You still might be able to bring charges against him for molestation. He could be tried for both," I say. "That way, he might never get out."

"I've thought about that. But after all these years it wouldn't change anything for me and only bring shame on my family."

Her recital of abuse continues. Even if I already didn't have my own suspicions about her stepfather, even if I weren't inclined to take a case like this, how could I refuse her? It looked like a lost cause from the get-go—trying to turn an accident or a suicide into a homicide. But lost causes are one of my specialties.

The pleasant amenities of flying first class keep coming, despite Marie's dark revelations. If only a scented steaming towel could wipe them away. Lunch is soon served: squash ratatouille for Marie and tenderloin of beef for me, followed by hot fudge sundaes prepared to order. Hearing out Marie doesn't leave me much appetite, but I sample everything. I may never fly this high again.

After eleven hours in the air we finally touch down at one in the afternoon in San Francisco. My body thinks it's bedtime. And it is, in Paris.

We clear customs, recheck our luggage, and prepare to lay over until our Honolulu flight. Marie waves a blue card that gets us into the airline's elite flyers lounge where we wait in relative comfort. She excuses herself to have another cigarette.

"A bad habit Pierre taught me," she says when she returns.

"He wasn't such a prince after all?"

"He was fine," Marie says. "I miss him. But smoking wasn't his only vice. Pierre had other women."

"So he was a philanderer, like your stepfather said?"

"Pierre wasn't devious. In fact, I wish he would have been a little less open about it. You saw some of his women."

"I did?"

"The nude paintings in our Rue Saint-Dominique bedroom."

"All of them?"

"Well, probably not all."

"And you were okay with that?"

"Actually, no. I was seriously thinking of leaving Pierre and coming back home to Hawai'i. But I didn't want to be anywhere near my stepfather."

"You're coming home now."

"Yes, to confront him. If all goes well, he'll finally pay for what he's done."

"That's a big 'if,'" I reply.

"I'll take that chance," she says.

Soon we board our flight to Honolulu. We're in first class again. Domestic first class. Not international. No sleeper seats. No champagne before takeoff. I hardly care. I look at all the fresh faces aboard primed for their Hawaiian vacations. All I want is sleep.

After we're in the air I keep awake long enough to ask Marie where she's staying on O'ahu.

"In Kailua," she says. "At Vivienne's house. She's so lovely. She's letting me use her car, too. Her caretaker will meet me in Kailua this evening."

"Once you're settled you may want to see friends you haven't seen for a while. That's natural. And I wouldn't think any of your friends would tell your stepfather you're back. But word gets around."

"I'm not planning to stay long—just long enough for you to complete your investigation. When can you get started? I can drive to your office tomorrow."

"Why don't I come to you?" I say. "The less you travel around the island the better. And I can check out the security of your accommodation."

"That would be easier for me." Marie gives me her cell number and the address of Vivienne's home in Kailua. We agree to meet there tomorrow morning at eleven, giving us a bit of time to recover. Then a flight attendant arrives with hot towels.

I don't remember much after this—except planting that steamy towel on my face—until the flight attendant awakens me to put my seatback forward for landing.

It's six in the evening in Honolulu. Six in the morning in Paris. No wonder I can't keep my eyes open.

three

Tuesday, April 9. I'm still floating over the white cliffs of Dover in my dreams when the chime of my cell phone awakens me.

A text from Kula's foster mom. "Can you stop by my cottage?" asks Maile Barnes. "We need to talk."

I can't imagine why the pet detective and I suddenly need to talk. We're old friends—well, we're more than that—but we haven't talked for weeks except to about Kula.

Maile is fostering the golden retriever because the Waikīkī Edgewater where I live doesn't allow pets. I adopted Kula from a client who has since taken up residence at Halawa Correctional Facility. Maile, a former K9 officer, was perfect for the job, especially when we were dating. Lately she's been seeing more of my old buddy in homicide, Frank Fernandez, than of me. She and Frank knew each other on the force, back when both of them were married. To other people, that is.

I struggle out of bed. I'm in that zombie-like state that descends on me after long-distance airline travel. This one is worse than usual—twelve time zones. I check my watch. Almost eight. I reply, "How about nine?"

"Fine," she texts back.

I shower, dress, grab a bowl of cereal, retrieve my car and head into Mānoa Valley. Pulling up in front of Maile's cottage I can tell right away something has changed. I can't put my finger on it. Then I hear growling—not one dog growling, but two. When I step from my car to her screen door I see Kula and another dog, a Rottweiler, going at it.

I don't bother to knock. I storm in and grab Kula by his collar, pull him away, and then stand between the golden retriever and the foaming Rottweiler. Maile rushes in, grabs the other dog, and says, "Blitz, no!"

Blood drips from my right hand. *Did the rottie get me?* I check. No, it's not me. It's Kula. His right ear is bleeding.

"Whose dog is this?" I ask Maile. "And why is he beefing with Kula?"

"They're usually okay together," she says.

"They're not okay," I say. "Not when Kula ends up bleeding."

"You know I'd never do anything to endanger Kula," she says a little defensively.

I check his ear more carefully. Just a nick. He probably doesn't need stitches. But he seems stunned. He sits silent and unmoving. "I've known some sweetheart Rottweilers. What's wrong with this one?"

Maile shrugs. "Playing for Blitz means nipping—and after a while Kula gets annoyed."

"I don't blame Kula. I'd get annoyed too," I say. "What is Blitz doing here?"

Maile gives me a look. "That's what I wanted to talk with you about, Kai. Frank and I are getting married."

It takes a moment for that sink in. Then I say, "Blitz is Frank's dog?"

She nods.

I glance into Maile's bedroom and see evidence of male clutter—cardboard boxes piled with a man's clothing and pairs of shoes and slippers under the bed.

Then I survey the living room. Kula's toys—rawhide chews, yellow-green tennis balls and braided tug ropes that are usually scattered about artfully—are ravaged and in disarray. It looks like a hurricane has hit. Kula used to live here like a prince. No more.

"Is Blitz staying?"

"That's the plan," Maile responds. "This doesn't happen very often. Kula and Blitz are still getting used to each other." The pet detective drags the Rottweiler outside.

I'm not convinced. I notice a dark red spot on Kula's other ear. This isn't the first time. No wonder the golden retriever doesn't seem his usually sunny self.

"Now that the skirmish is over," Maile says when she returns without the Rottweiler, "sit down, Kai, and let's talk."

Soon we are occupying her two rattan chairs opposite one another. The retriever curls up on a throw rug by my feet. Kula's ear has stopped bleeding, but bright red drips still dot his coat. I turn to Maile, whose spunky independent nature I've always admired and sometimes run afoul of. I remember how her face used to light up when she saw me.

Maile now looks me up and down dispassionately and says, "Are you okay?"

"As okay as anybody could be after spending twenty-four hours in airplanes and airports."

"I mean are you okay about Frank and me getting married?"

"No worries," I say. "You have to do what's right for you." I gaze under her bed again at Frank's slippers.

"I care about you, Kai," she says. "You know I do. But we could never quite work things out."

"My fault," I say.

"Not you," Maile replies. "*Us.* We just didn't click."

"So you and Frank . . . you click?"

She nods. "I think so. Frank and I are a couple of veteran cops who see things pretty much the same way. You'd never guess it. I mean, we seem so different on the surface."

"You do," I say. "I'd never have put the two of you together. But whatever makes you happy."

The conversation goes on like this, Maile trying her best not to hurt my feelings and also blaming herself more than she should. I'm grateful, whatever her motive. But my thoughts keep returning to Kula and how to get him away from Blitz. I believe Maile when she says she'd never intentionally endanger Kula, but her pending marriage to Frank seems to have clouded her vision.

When we finally wrap up I say, "How about the golden boy and I hit the waves today?"

"That'll be great," she says. "And give him a break from Blitz."

I reach down and stroke the sunny retriever who is still curled up by my feet. "Kula, wanna go surfing?"

He perks up. Before long I'm gathering cousin Alika's tandem board from Maile's garage and Kula is hopping into my car.

Driving down the valley, I glance over at the retriever, his head out the window and flashing his goofy smile. He's happy again. I see once more those red spots on his coat.

That decides it. Kula's not returning to Maile's cottage.

I check my watch. Before it gets any later in the morning I've got to make a difficult phone call. Not about Kula.

About my client's deceased mother. I pull over and punch in the familiar number. The phone rings three times and then I hear his deep, gravelly voice: "Fernandez, Homicide."

"Hi Frank. It's Kai Cooke."

There's a long pause.

"Congratulations." I fill the silence. "I hear you and Maile are getting married."

"That's big of you, Kai." Frank sounds impatient. "So what can I do for you?"

"You investigated the death of Mrs. Beatrice Ho at Makapu'u?"

"Right," he says. "Nice lady. What a shame."

"I'm representing a Ho family member. She's an attractive twenty-something"—I try to entice him without using Marie's name—"who wants to hear about the investigation. It would be doing me a big favor, Frank, if you would meet with us, maybe this afternoon?"

"Kind of busy, Kai."

"How about lunch? The meal is on me. Where would you like to eat?"

"The Wharf is good." He's referring to a seafood restaurant on the waterfront near Ward Avenue, not far from HPD headquarters on Beretania Street.

"The Wharf it is, Frank." I say. "We'll meet you there at noon."

I'm surprised, once I hang up, that Frank agreed. Maybe he feels guilty about marrying Maile? I recall the last time I saw Fernandez, nearly a year ago, when he was interviewing two suspects from my investigation of Ryan Song's hanging in Paris. Their names were Scooter and Brad—a couple of fine young lads. *Not.*

I aim my old Chevy over the Pali Highway. Rolling into Kailua town a few minutes later I check the address my new client gave me. It's in a quiet, secluded beachside neighborhood of coconut palms and putting-green lawns. Vivienne's rambling ranch home in a shady cul-de-sac is large by Oʻahu standards with a tropically landscaped yard. She did well in her divorce.

I pull into a circular driveway. On the front *lānai* Marie is reclining in a lounge chair, smoking. She rises and waves, looking amazingly fresh considering the journey we both just endured. She's young.

I open the car door and Kula jumps out. First thing he does is water the perfectly clipped grass. Then he rolls on that manicured green, moaning in ecstasy, sunshine flooding his golden coat. When I walk toward the house he snaps to his feet and follows me.

Marie snuffs out her cigarette and she says, "Oh, what a gorgeous retriever!"

Kula prances onto the porch and makes a beeline for Marie. He sits in front of her and gives her that melting brown-eyed retriever look that says, "How can you resist me?"

Truth is, she can't. Marie hugs him and plants her nose against his.

"Where did you get this beautiful boy?" she asks.

"Long story," I reply. "I didn't know you were a dog person."

"We had two poodles before my mother died. My stepfather packed them off while I was at college. I can never forgive him for that, either."

While she's stroking Kula I eye the smoldering butt of her cigarette.

Marie sees me and says, "I haven't smoked in the house. I just assumed Vivienne preferred I didn't."

"Safe assumption," I say. And then: "Nice place, huh?"

"It's really cute," Marie replies. "Let me show you around." She leads me in the front door.

A cool breeze wafts through open jalousies over comfy furnishings and gleaming hardwood floors. In the cozy den I see evidence of her Sadie that Vivienne lost to divorce—a tartan plaid dog bed, stainless food and water dishes, assorted stuffed animals, chews, and toys, and even a doggie door leading to a backyard swimming pool. Hanging on the wall is the framed photo of the chocolate Labrador.

Kula takes a stuffed Mallard duck that once was Sadie's into his mouth and curls up on her tartan bed.

"Your dog really knows how to make himself at home," Marie says.

"He's good at that," I say. "Speaking of Kula, would you mind him staying with you for a few days?" I explain why Kula can't stay with me at the Edgewater.

"That would be super," Marie responds.

"Great." I snap a photo of Kula on Sadie's bed and text it to Vivienne in Paris, where it's closing in on eleven at night. "Okay if my dog Kula stays in your home for a while with Marie?"

Less than a minute later my phone chimes: "I love him already! Will he be there when I return?"

"Could be arranged," I text back.

That problem solved, Marie and I sit in the den while Kula snoozes. I explain to Marie that we have a lunch appointment with Homicide Detective Frank Fernandez this afternoon and if we're lucky he might share with us details from his investigation into her mother's death.

I tell Marie about the usual terms for my investigations, but I defer the retainer for now. I know she's good for it. Plus she's agreed to keep Kula.

Marie tries to give me, as her stepfather did, a bundle of euros. I wave her off.

"My first-class ticket from Paris alone must have cost you more than my usual retainer," I say.

"You're sure?" she asks.

I nod but then wonder if I'll later regret not taking those euros.

four

Soon we're heading over the Pali into Honolulu to meet Frank Fernandez, leaving Kula lounging in Vivienne's den. When we arrive at The Wharf the harbor is calm as glass. There's barely a breeze.

Marie and I are led to a booth overlooking the water. The Wharf's ambience is seashore and maritime. Our spar-varnished table looks right out of a ship's galley. A waitress leaves three menus. I gaze at the placid harbor, reflecting the perfect circle of the April sun. Will Frank be half this placid? Maybe, now that he's engaged to the pet detective.

Before he arrives I ask Marie not to mention Kula. She agrees.

At about ten minutes after noon—not especially late for Fernandez—the big man lumbers in, his huge frame filling the doorway. Even seeing him at this distance reminds me, if I need reminding, you don't want to mess with Frank Fernandez.

As he approaches I notice a folder in his hands—hopefully pertaining to the investigation of Mrs. Ho's death. His usual scowl has been replaced by a faint smile. He checks out the young woman sitting next to me at the table and his smile deepens. He likes what he sees.

"Howzit, Kai?" he asks as he lowers himself into the booth next to Marie. He's got to be twice her size. The contrast is almost comical. Almost. Frank can be a grizzly bear or a teddy bear, depending on his mood. Today he seems to be feeling warm and cuddly.

"Fine," I respond, whiffing his spicy aftershave. "Frank Fernandez, meet Marie Ho."

He turns toward her and stretches out his huge mitt, though he doesn't offer it to me. Her hand disappears into his momentarily and then reappears. "Very sorry about your mother," he says. "I investigated her death at Makapu'u. But I guess Kai told you that already."

"Thank you for seeing us," Marie responds. "I'd be grateful for anything you can tell me."

"Glad to," Frank responds, in the spirit of cooperation I hoped for. "But it looks like we're going to order lunch first."

He's right. The waitress is back and we quickly scan our menus.

Frank already knows what he wants—the most expensive entrée, seared *ahi*. And a draft beer. He must be off duty. Marie orders a watercress salad and iced tea. Can she live on that? And I order a *mahi* sandwich and fries.

The waitress departs and returns before long with our drinks. Frank gets right into his beer, sipping the foam off the head. He catches a bit of foam on his upper lip. I motion to him and he wipes and seems grateful.

"I remember the investigation all too well." Frank sips his beer. "I was going through my divorce and was in misery. Anyway, everyone knows your mother was a fine and generous lady, Marie. But few people know what you probably do, that she suffered bouts of depression after your father and brother died, which led to her becoming your stepfather's patient. We learned from Dr. Grimes that she often visited Makapu'u near where your brother lost his life in that surfing accident. Bereaved people often do. They sometimes hold vigils and build informal shrines."

Fernandez's monologue is interrupted by the return of the waitress laden with three oval platters bearing our lunches. In front of Marie she puts a mound of greenery that would make a bunny's eyes pop. Next comes Fernandez's seared *ahi* and all the trimmings. And my *mahi* sandwich.

Before Marie takes a first bite of watercress, she says to the homicide detective: "My stepfather had reason to want my mother dead."

Fernandez puts down his *ahi*. "When a woman dies under questionable circumstances, the first person of interest we interview is her husband or boyfriend. And I can assure you that your stepfather was thoroughly investigated."

"And what did you find?" I ask.

"Dr. Grimes was on Moloka'i at the time of your mother's death." Frank nods to Marie. "He was in the Moloka'i Beach Hotel register. Hotel personnel say they saw him there that night and the next morning."

"Who are they?" she asks.

"It's all in the report. A chambermaid, a bartender, and a dockhand who took care of the doctor's boat." Fernandez pulls out that folder he carried in with him. "This is a closed case. Otherwise, I couldn't share the file with you. You may not want to look at the photos," he says to Marie. "These copies are for Kai."

He hands me the folder. I open it a crack and peek in. The photos are of Beatrice Ho. Bloated, bruised, and cut.

"She was in the water by midnight, maybe earlier," Frank says. "That's the closest our medical examiner could come. Her body was found early the next morning. We pulled her out about 7:30 am. She didn't die from drowning. She struck the ridge a few times on the way down."

Marie reaches for the folder. "I want to see." She scans the photos. Instead of tearing up, her face becomes tight.

"So she could have died anytime midnight or before?" I ask Frank.

"Right."

"That gives Dr. Grimes time to make his way from Moloka'i, if he didn't have an alibi."

"Yeah, technically he could," Frank says, "but not likely. Dr. Grimes is disabled. He has a limp and walks with a cane."

"He's not as disabled as he lets on," Marie says. "He secretly delights in snagging those special parking spots from people who truly need them."

Frank raises his brows. "Anyway, after a thorough investigation we dropped Dr. Grimes as a person of interest. Finally, all available evidence pointed to an accident or suicide. Since there were no witnesses and no note, her case was ruled an unattended death."

"What about Grimes' boat?" I ask.

"We know he took his boat out early that morning, per his usual weekend routine. He didn't deny that."

"And the night before—when she died?"

"Think about it, Kai. He can maybe get the boat over to O'ahu in the dark of night—though the Moloka'i Channel is no picnic—but where would he dock and what would he use for ground transportation? The bus?"

I shrug.

"We can trace those things. There was nothing to trace. Plus we found Mrs. Ho's car parked near where she plunged from the cliff, as we expected. If he drove her there, how would Dr. Grimes get back to his boat?"

"An accomplice?" I suggest. "Or maybe she drove herself there first and he drove another car later and surprised her? After all, he knew his wife might be there."

Then Marie says, "Or he put his mountain bike in the trunk of her car and then he pedaled back from the cliffs to his boat."

"It's plausible," I reply. My phone chimes. I silence it.

Then Frank says, "It has to be painful to lose your mother at your young age, Marie. You may not know that she had reasons to be despondent besides the losses of your father and brother."

"So you think she jumped?" I ask.

"I didn't say that," Fernandez replies. "I'm just saying that if she did she had reasons."

"What reasons?" Marie asks.

"One was Davidson Loretta, a young lawyer she was very fond of."

"Dave Loretta?" Marie asks. "Her former trust attorney?"

"Right. Loretta came to see her, at her request, on the day she died to discuss changes to her will. When Loretta arrived Mrs. Ho was very upset. She had just found out that he had been skimming funds to cover his gambling losses. Whether she threatened to turn him in, we don't know. Loretta said not. He told us he promised to pay back every penny and she seemed satisfied. We had no way to verify that. Main thing, it was a major betrayal of your mother by a man she thought of as almost family."

"Did you consider him a suspect?" I ask.

Fernandez scratches his head. "Loretta had an alibi—a late dinner that night at the Halekūlani with a friend. We interviewed the friend and he verified."

"Why did Mrs. Ho want to change her will?"

"We don't know. And if Loretta knew he didn't tell."

Marie nudges me and whispers, *"I know."*

I ask Fernandez, "What other reasons?"

He turns to Marie, frowns apologetically, and says, "Mrs. Ho's second husband had a lover. The family dog-walker. A fortyish blonde named Krystal."

"My stepfather and Krystal?" Marie's face reddens.

"Did you know her?" Fernandez asks.

"Krystal helped with our two poodles," Marie explains. "She seemed nice. Was I ever wrong!"

"Apparently, your mother fired her after figuring out something was going on between the dog walker and your stepfather," Fernandez continues. "What I didn't know until I met Krystal in person was that she's a former body builder. Still had muscles, despite not being in her prime. We dug a little deeper and found an assault conviction. She whacked another woman pretty badly and got herself a long probation. I guess your family didn't do a background check on her?"

"Was Krystal a suspect in Mrs. Ho's death?" I ask.

"The night she died, the dog walker had an alibi. She was at a rock concert at the Blaisdell Arena. Ticket stub to prove it. Her friends verified."

"What concert?" I ask.

"Yes." Fernandez says.

"Yes, what?" I ask.

"You know—*Yes*—the British band."

"Oh."

"I don't believe Dave Loretta or Krystal killed my mother," Marie says. "My stepfather did. I want Kai to prove it."

"It's your money," Fernandez says. "You can spend it however you like."

"If Kai traces my stepfather's movements on that night and his alibis fall apart, then we'll know. We'll put him on O'ahu and we'll have our killer."

"We already covered that territory," Fernandez says. "If you want Kai to go over it again, like I said, it's your money. But in the end I think you're going to find that your mother's death was unattended, just as our investigation found."

"No way," she says defiantly.

I step in. "Good of you, Frank, to take us into your confidence like this."

The tab for lunch comes just as Fernandez is rising to leave.

"Thanks," he says. "They grill a nice piece of fish here."

five

After lunch when I 'm walking with Marie to my car I un-silence my cell phone. It chimes again.

A text from Dr. Grimes: "Must see you immediately when you return from Paris. Urgent. GJG."

I show the message to Marie.

"What are you going to tell him?"

"Nothing now. If I was still in Paris it would be after midnight. He can't expect to hear from me right away. "He doesn't know I'm here."

"I definitely don't want him to know I'm in Hawai'i," Marie says. "The thought is chilling."

"No worries," I say. "What did you want to tell me at The Wharf about your mother's will?"

"I'm sure she intended to cut my stepfather out completely— after she confronted him about what he did to me."

"An even stronger motive for murder?"

"Exactly. But I guess she felt so disgusted by Dave Loretta's betrayal that she decided to find another attorney to change her will. She never got the chance. She died that night."

On the drive back over the Pali Highway to Kailua we talk more about what we learned from Fernandez.

"Could Loretta's betrayal," I ask Marie, "have caused your mother to jump?"

"She was fond of him. But he didn't mean *that* much to her."

"And what about Krystal, the dog walker?"

"I'm blown away she had a criminal record."

"Would she have been strong enough to push your mother off a cliff?"

"Maybe. But she didn't. My stepfather did."

"Ordinarily I would investigate Krystal and Loretta, just to remove them from our list."

"You only need to investigate my stepfather."

"If that's what you want," I say. "But if HPD turned up nothing to implicate him, I may turn up nothing too."

"It was convenient for the police to rule my mother's murder an unattended death."

"Frank Fernandez is no slouch. He may not always get it right, but he does more often than not. He's been at this for years and, I have to admit, he's good at it."

"He doesn't know my stepfather like I do." She smiles sarcastically.

"Okay, we'll presume Dr. Grimes pushed your mother and we'll try to find evidence that he did."

"I'm as sure about her end as I am about Pierre's."

"We'll see," I say.

When I drop Marie in Kailua, Kula is wild to see us. I walk him to the beach and let him swim. He's soaked and sandy and calm when we return. I rinse him with a garden hose and dry him with some beach towels I find in a bin by Vivienne's pool. He seems content to stay with Marie when I drive to my office.

Chinatown is quiet this afternoon. The usual odors from sidewalks and gutters along Maunakea Street are tempered by the waning April sun. Inside the flower shop Mrs. Fujiyama stands at the cash register with a customer purchasing three orchid *lei*. At the work table Blossom and Joon are stringing pink plumeria. Their perfume takes me back to Paris. I think of Vivienne, but try not to dwell. The wait until May will be hard enough.

I head up the orange shag stairs and walk past the psychedelic bead curtain of our resident psychic, Madame Zenobia. Shirley—her real name—has a client. I'm home free. Less than a week ago she foretold my unplanned trip to Paris. Did she really see France in her crystal ball? *Whatevahs.* I brought her a postcard from the Eiffel Tower. It can wait.

In my office I'm about to drop off from colossal jet lag but manage to do something I'd like to avoid even more than figuring my taxes, postponed by my Paris trip. I reach over the pile of forms and receipts on my desk for my phone and punch in the pet detective's number. I'm several hours late returning Kula already and she's probably worrying.

The first thing she says is, "Where's Kula?"

"In a safe place," I respond. "Away from Blitz."

"You have no right, Kai." She wastes no words. "You're breaking my heart."

I remind her that I was entrusted with Kula's care by his previous owner. I thank her for giving Kula a safe and comfortable home. Up to now.

"What do you mean, 'up to now'?" she asks.

"There's no safety or comfort in your cottage for Kula as long as Blitz is there."

"Where's Kula?" she asks again.

"With a trusted friend, a few blocks from the beach." I don't say which friend or which beach. "I'll be dropping in on him every day—and taking him surfing regularly."

"If this is a ploy to win me back from Frank," she says, "it's so cynical and cruel. To hold Kula hostage like this, Kai—I can't believe you'd do it."

"It's not a ploy."

"I believed you when you said you were okay with my marrying Frank. But obviously you're not okay."

"I wish you both well. I'm already moving on."

"That's not how you're behaving."

The conversation goes on like this. Then things get worse. She starts crying and through her tears says, *"I thought you were my friend!"* She hangs up.

I feel like a heel.

I look at the clock. Four in the afternoon in Honolulu. Four in the morning in Paris. I drive to the Waikīkī Edgewater and crash on my bed. And I don't get up again until early the next morning.

six

Wednesday, April 10. I'm one of about four dozen passengers aboard a 9:05 am flight to the Friendly Isle. My boarding pass lists my destination as (MKK) MOLOKAʻI — HOʻOLEHUA, the name of the tiny airport there. Back when I did my first investigation on Molokaʻi I flew on an eighteen-seat Twin-Otter, operated by Island Hopper airlines. Today's twin turbo-prop commuter planes are roomier, quieter, and smoother, making the journey to Molokaʻi a little less, well, thrilling.

As the airplane taxis to the runway I start to see similarities between this new case and the one I worked back then. In both there was a death from a fall. Sara Ridgely-Parke, the victim in the murder on Molokaʻi, plunged from the cliffs at Kalaupapa and Mrs. Beatrice Ho from the cliffs at Makapuʻu. The first death was ruled an accident, the second unattended. In both cases my clients, Adrienne Ridgley then and Marie Ho now, hired me to prove that the victim's end did not stem from an accident or suicide, but from murder.

As for the new case, if it weren't for what I know about Dr. Grimes that Frank Fernandez doesn't, I might be swayed by the homicide detective's conclusion. But I'm not being paid to agree with Frank. I'm being paid to prove he was wrong. To find anything he and his crew missed, however, will be a challenge. I can't kid myself about that.

When the airplane hums down the runway and climbs over the white sands of Waikīkī Beach, I'm wishing I was down there carving frothy trails in the turquoise surf. But at least up here I'm getting paid. I think so, anyway.

Should I have taken those euros? Then I reassure myself. She's an heiress—she's good for it.

Leaving Oʻahu behind, the airliner crosses the wind-whipped Kaʻiwi Channel—twenty-five miles of whitecaps between Oʻahu and Molokaʻi. If Marie is right and her stepfather pushed her mother, Dr. Grimes would have had to pilot his boat in darkness across this wild channel, do the deed, and then return again before first light.

Very difficult. But not impossible.

I've already checked conditions for the crossing from Molokaʻi to Oʻahu on the night Beatrice Ho died.

Calm. One night past a full moon.

If Dr. Grimes wanted to return secretly to Oʻahu to murder his wife, this would have been the perfect night. He'd really have to scoot both ways for the timing to work out. And he could in his speedboat.

I peer out the window at the dark sea below. It's amazing how the milky turquoise reef waters near shore around our islands so suddenly turn blue-black as India ink in our deeper channels.

The dark blues lighten again as the airplane descends over Molokaʻi's West End—an arid cocoa brown and rust-red plateau of stunted *kiawe,* grazing cattle, and a two-lane highway with a few rusty side roads. The wheels of the airliner fold down and before long brush the macadam strip at Hoʻolehua Airport.

I disembark, collect my rental car, and turn east onto a narrow blacktop—well, more red than black—that stretches though more of the same terrain to Kaunakakai. Within minutes, I'm there.

Kaunakakai, the Friendly Isle's main town, seems frozen in time. It's like I never left. And still not a single stoplight! The three short blocks of tin roofed mom-and-pop stores with hitching posts couldn't be more familiar.

I drive through town behind a rusty pickup with the bumper sticker: "Don't Change Molokaʻi; Let Molokaʻi Change You." That says it all.

On my earlier case I stayed at the ʻUkulele Inn, whose lively Banyan Tree Bar kept me up more nights than I'd like to remember. But the storied old inn with its funky oceanfront cottages has closed down since then. Only one full-service establishment remains near Kaunakakai and the harbor where the doctor kept his boat. The Molokaʻi Beach Hotel.

According to the report Fernandez gave me, the doctor's alibi for the night his wife died was confirmed by a chambermaid who saw him early the next morning, by a bartender who served him on the evening before, and by his boat caretaker who confirmed the doctor's watercraft was docked in its accustomed place that evening. For the period between the late evening and the early morning HPD apparently relied on the doctor's word.

Or, to put it another way, Fernandez and his crew could find no evidence that the doctor wasn't where he said he was.

I made some calls before leaving Oʻahu to ensure the chambermaid, bartender, and dockhand would be available.

The first two, Moloka'i Beach Hotel employees, probably don't know I'm coming. The third, an independent contractor, does. I hope all three can tell me something they didn't tell HPD.

I drive about two miles outside of Kaunakakai to the Moloka'i Beach, whose Polynesian thatched cottages and island-style ambience mark a pleasant departure from the typical high-rise hotel. I wander by a few of the outlying cottages on my way to the open-air lobby at the water's edge. A sign by the front desk announces Moloka'i-style music performed every weekend, with a photo of a group of *kupuna,* or elders, strumming ukuleles and guitars and singing. *Kanekapila.*

Pumping through the lobby's loudspeakers is my favorite song about Moloka'i, written by Larry Helm and performed by Ehukai:

> *Take me back . . . take me back . . .*
> *Back to da kine.*
> *All over, mo' bettah,*
> *Moloka'i. I will return.*

I give a smiling desk attendant my card and ask where I might find Lena, the chambermaid. The attendant tells me Lena is cleaning beachfront cottages and shows me on a hotel map.

As I head for the cottages my phone rings.

Caller ID says HPD. I answer and hear the gravelly voice of Homicide Detective Frank Fernandez. Yesterday his tone was calm and almost sweet. Today more edgy.

"I've got to tell you, Kai, you shouldn't have taken that yellow dog from Maile. That was a low thing to do."

I gather he's referring to Kula. If I didn't need Fernandez's cooperation on this case I'd simply tell him the retriever is mine. End of story.

"Maile wants to know when he's coming home. She misses him and so does Blitz. Those two dogs are inseparable."

"They were fighting when I saw them," I reply. "Blitz drew blood."

"Hey, they're dogs, Kai. What do you expect?"

"A hostile environment isn't good for either of them."

"Well, we have a difference of opinion about that, my friend."

"So we do," I say

Frank hangs up.

seven

I follow the hotel map, wander a bit and finally find a cottage with the door open to a housekeeping cart. I knock and walk in. It's a simple shoebox room, airy and bright, with a sliding glass door to a *lānai* at the water's edge. A bone-thin *haole* woman with a grey bun is mopping the bathroom floor.

"Lena, Detective Fernandez gave me your name," I say. "I've come from Honolulu to ask you just a few questions. Okay?"

She turns to me, surprised. "Questions about what?" Her English sounds more mainland than local.

I pull out a photo of the doctor from the internet. "Dr. Grimes used to be a regular guest here and Detective Fernandez said you knew him."

"And who are you?"

"I'm a private detective." I show her my card. "I worked on Moloka'i a few years ago—the case of the woman who fell from the Kalaupapa cliffs."

"Oh, the mule ride accident?" Lena's expression changes.

"That's the one. It wasn't an accident."

She puts down her mop and glances at the photo. "Yes, I knew him. I already told the detective everything I could remember."

I nod. "You told Detective Fernandez Dr. Grimes was in his hotel room the morning after his wife died, is that right?"

"That's what I told him."

"How did you know the doctor was here?"

"He hung a DO NOT DISTURB sign on his door. He said he had taken his boat out early that morning and was catching up on sleep. That's probably why he was still in his room when I came around ten."

"So ten in the morning is the first time you saw him?"

"A little after, yes."

"And you believed he was in his room all night?"

"That's what he told me."

"Did you see him here that night?"

"I'm not here at night. Just in the mornings and early afternoons when I clean rooms."

"Okay," I say. "Did anything strike you as different about the doctor's stay on this particular night, on this particular weekend?"

"No—" Lena hesitates. "Well, yes. He was alone."

"He wasn't always?"

"It's none of my business," she says. "Really."

"Who was usually with him?"

Lena says nothing.

"On that night he was alone?" I try again. "But on most nights when he stayed here he was not alone?"

Lena slowly nods. She's saying yes and at the same time she's saying she feels uncomfortable saying yes.

"Did you mention this to Detective Fernandez?"

"He didn't ask."

"Mahalo," I say. "You've been a big help."

I say goodbye to Lena, wondering why Fernandez didn't pick up on the fact that Dr. Grimes usually had company during his weekends on Molokaʻi. But not on the weekend his wife died. Then I remember. Fernandez was going through a divorce. He said he was in misery. And maybe drinking more than usual. Frank wasn't at his best.

Now it starts to make sense. Why else would the doctor spend frequent weekends on Molokaʻi? He didn't fish. He didn't hunt. He didn't hula. And there were probably as many opportunities in waters around Oʻahu as around the Friendly Isle to run his speedboat.

Dr. Grimes came here to be with her. The dog walker. The muscular blonde. Krystal was attending a rock concert on the evening Beatrice Ho died. And that left him alone on Molokaʻi. Or so the story went.

It's lunchtime now. I head not to the hotel's restaurant but to its oceanfront bar. On the way my phone chimes. A text from Vivienne.

"Hello, Kai. Paris TV news is reporting three persons of interest in the hit-and-run case of Pierre Garneaux. One in Lyon, France, and two in Honolulu, Hawaiʻi. Thought you should know. Miss you, Vivienne."

Two in Honolulu? So now I'm on the short list with Dr. Grimes?

What went down in Paris seems worlds away from Molokaʻi. But these two distant worlds are suddenly converging.

I reply to Vivienne, "Thanks. Miss you too."

I step up to the oceanfront bar overlooking ripples lapping the shore and order a beer. The nametag on the bartender, a local guy about my age, says Elton. Just the man I want to talk to. As he pulls the tap and slides a frothy mug across the bar, we talk story in Pidgin above the lunch-hour bustle of the nearby restaurant.

We're wrapping up a rundown of surf spots on the Friendly Isle when I show him the photo of Dr. Grimes and ask: "Eh, Elton, you remembah dis' guy? He come hea on da weekends—regular kine. One *haole* doctor, mid-fifties. He from O'ahu.   Got one fas' boat, brah, ovah in da harbor."

The bartender studies the photo. "Yeah, I remembah. Wuz long time ago. Da guy's wife wen' fall off one cliff, yeah?"

"Das da guy," I say. "T'ink he hea in da hotel da night his wife fall?"

"Dunno, brah. I see him dat night in da bar, li' I tell da police. But how I know where he spend da night?   I not hea all night."

"Das da t'ing," I say. "Wuz he hea or wuz he dere?"

The bartender shrugs.

"What you t'ink?   Maybe da doctor push her off da cliff at Makapu'u?"

"Not if he on Moloka'i, brah."

I change course. "Da doctor get one *wahine* wit' him mos' weekends, yeah?"

"Ho, how can forget!" Elton lights up. "I wen' see him all da time sitting at da bar wit' da *wahine*."

"You remembah what she look like?"

"Beeg muscles, brah. She one body-builder or somet'ing li' dat."

"Was," I say. "Why you no tell police about da *wahine*?"

"She not hea dat weekend, brah. Das why."

"T'anks, eh?" I say, rising from the bar. "If you t'ink of anyt'ing else, try call me, 'kay?"

From my wallet I hand him my card and then set a twenty on the bar under my frothy mug. He glances at the chiseled face of Andrew Jackson. Elton's own face brightens. I guess he likes Jackson's rugged good looks.

eight

Walking away, I consider what I've learned so far. Chambermaid Lena tells me nothing that Fernandez didn't except she mentions that Dr. Grimes was alone on that fateful weekend, implying his being alone was unusual. Then bartender Elton confirms the company the doctor kept on his lost weekends was none other than Krystal, the dog walker fired by his wife Beatrice Ho. So already I know something that Fernandez either didn't know or didn't tell me.

It's curious that Dr. Grimes brought the blonde body builder with him most weekends to Moloka'i but not the weekend his wife died. Krystal had an alibi—a rock concert on O'ahu. Could she have slipped away undetected and been an accomplice to murder? In any case, so far Grimes has no iron clad alibi that he was on Moloka'i that night.

Two down and one to go.

From the thatched cottages of the Moloka'i Beach Hotel I drive two short miles back to Kaunakakai. I go barely a quarter mile beyond to the water's edge and pull onto a long wharf—the longest in the state—jutting for what seems like a half mile into brilliant blue Kaunakakai Harbor. The wharf culminates in what is known as Pier Island—an oblong dock for inter-island barges, ferries, fishing boats and pleasure craft.

I park in one of the open stalls by the pier's entrance and step into a balmy breeze. Across from the harbor is a sweeping view to the southeast of the cloud-capped verdant islands of Lana'i and Maui. And in the foreground, moored at the pier, a dozen colorful boats gleam like lollipops in the sun. I search for the one formerly owned by Dr. Grimes, recalling the model the doctor showed me of his sleek racer. When I suggested he could cross the Moloka'i Channel in no time, he agreed, but only on those rare days when conditions were right. Otherwise, he would have been in for a rough ride.

The channel that separates the islands of Moloka'i and O'ahu—whose traditional name is Ka'iwi or "Channel of Bones"—has a reputation for bashing boats. Open ocean swells pushing through the narrow canyon between the two islands and churned up by foul weather have wrought destruction on unwary mariners since the beginning of recorded history. It was in this treacherous channel that one of Hawai'i's most famous and legendary watermen, Eddie Aikau, was lost.

But on the night Dr. Grimes's wife died seas were calm and the moon nearly full. He could have roared across the channel, docked near his Portlock home, and then orchestrated his wife's plunge from the cliffs of Makapu'u.

Scanning the dock I spot it—long and sleek and shaped like an expensive cigar. The hull is emblazoned with orange flames—fitting for a water-borne rocket—and floodlights grace the bow for running at night. I walk to the stern to verify: SEA YA LATER.

The guy I need to talk to ought to be here any minute. Ikaika is his name. From a boathouse on the *makai* end of the pier a man ambles toward me. He looks older than I expected and walks a bit hunched over. Fernandez's report indicated that Ikaika makes his living caring for boats of absentee owners like the doctor.

"Sorry," Ikaika says when he reaches me, "I stay on Hawaiian time."

"No worries," I say, checking out his silver Fu Manchu mustache and skin tanned as reddish-brown as *koa*. He's got to be well past sixty. "Jus' get here myself. Ikaika, you like tell me 'bout Dr. Grimes and his boat?"

"Fo' sure," Ikaika replies. "Know da doctor fo' long time, brah. He wen come here on da weekends. Otherwise, his boat jus' sit here at da dock."

"On da night his wife die on O'ahu, you remembah, a few years ago? Da detective ask you about 'um."

"Long time ago, brah."

"Maybe I jus' ask you da same questions? Maybe you remembah somet'ing new?"

"Dunno, brah. Long time."

"Okay, on da night da doctor's wife wen fall from da cliffs on Makapu'u, wuz da doctor's boat here?"

"When I leave dat night, da boat still here, brah. Wuz almos' dark, yeah?"

"What time you come back da next morning?"

"Early, brah. Maybe seven."

"Da doctor's boat still here?"

"No, but he cruise in pretty soon aftah I get here. Da doctor like take his boat out early in da morning—dawn patrol, you know?—when da water smooth and glassy. He like go fas'.   Dat morning no different, like I wen tell da detective."

"Maybe da doctor take da boat out da night befo'. Maybe he gone all night?"

"Could have, brah. But didn't."

I take another tack. "Ikaika, how long you t'ink it take da doctor to drive da boat to Oʻahu?"

"Oh, long time, brah." The old man explains that the shortest distance between the islands of Molokaʻi and Oʻahu is about twenty-six miles, but from Kaunakakai Harbor to the closest small boat harbor on Oʻahu is much farther. More like forty-five miles. "And da Kaʻiwi Channel get really rough, brah. Hit one big wave and peel yo' eyebrows back, fo' sure."

"Dat night was calm, yeah?"

"Long time. Doan remembah."

Ikaika seems to be having repeated memory lapses. I ask him a few more questions with similar results and then say, "T'anks, eh?" and shake his hand local style.

"No mention, brah," he says and slowly ambles away.

Ikaika has told me nothing he didn't already tell Fernandez and his crew, but from the old salt's convenient forgetfulness and omissions it could be he's not telling all.

On my late afternoon flight back to Honolulu I sort through what I've learned from my three interviews. Dr. Grimes had the means and the motive and the opportunity to cross the channel that night in moonlight and in calm seas to murder his wife. I cannot yet prove he did this. But I can say that he could have done it.

After the plane lands and I'm driving home I get a call on my cellphone from the doctor himself. He leaves a message that I listen to once I'm back at the Waikīkī Edgewater.

"I've been contacted by Paris Police, via HPD, about the hit-and-run death of Marie's boyfriend. I expect my own stepdaughter has implicated me and I'm not happy about it. I'd like your full report when you return from Paris. And don't be surprised if you hear from Paris Police too. GJG."

nine

The next morning, Thursday, April 11, I text Dr. Grimes that I will get my report to him as soon as possible. For all he knows I'm still in Paris. And his daughter is too.

By mid-morning I'm driving to Kailua. When I pull into Vivienne's place Marie is on the *lānai* enjoying a little taste of home—that packed-rice and sliced meat local delicacy wrapped in dried seaweed called Spam *musubi*. Kula sits attentively beside her waiting for a bite. She doesn't disappoint him. No surprise the retriever misses my arrival. But Marie doesn't and points him in my direction. He dashes to me.

I get my warm and fuzzy fix and then fill Marie in on my investigation. She's not surprised that Dr. Grimes' alibis are full of holes. The more I tell her, the angrier she gets. She tosses what's left of her Spam musubi, wrapper and all, into a waste basket. Kula heads that way, but I grab him by the collar.

"My own mother's horrid death wouldn't be too good for my stepfather."

"The stiffest sentence under Hawai'i law," I remind her, "is life in prison. And in France I doubt they still employ the guillotine."

Marie perks up. "That would be perfect for him. Off with his head!"

We move on to the hard part. We have reason to believe Dr. Grimes may in fact have piloted his boat to O'ahu on the night her mother died, but we don't yet have proof. We need evidence that shows he actually did.

"If your stepfather made the crossing that night he would need to dock near your home in Portlock. Any idea where?"

"Let me think," she says.

"Take your time," I reply.

She does. But before long she says, "His former partner, Dr. Kitagawa, has two boat slips. Dr. Kitagawa and my stepfather had a disagreement and they no longer practice together. I don't think they even speak to one another anymore. But before that happened my stepfather occasionally used one of Dr. Kitagawa's slips."

"Where are Dr. Kitagawa's boat slips?" I ask. "Anywhere close to your family home?"

"In Hawai'i Kai Marina," she says. "Only about a mile from where I grew up."

"Sounds like we need to talk to Dr. Kitagawa. Can we do that?"

"We can try," she replies. "I might still have his number in my phone contacts." She checks. "Yes, I do."

"Let's give the doctor a call."

She punches in his number. I overhear ringing and then a faint "Hello." Marie identifies herself and Dr. Kitagawa is apparently happy to hear from her, based on the small talk that follows. Soon Marie is thanking him and saying she looks forward to seeing him.

"He's home and he'll see us as soon as we get there," Marie says.

We put Kula in the house and head for my car. Before we climb in I look back and he's peering through a den window with a sad look. I screw up my courage and mouth, "Sorry boy."

His melting brown eyes turn from sad to desolate.

Predictably I cave in. "Okay, c'mon."

Before long we're rolling with the golden retriever's head in the breeze wearing that goofy smile.

We pass through Waimānalo and then around Makapu'u Point, where Marie's mother lost her life, into the arid southern tip of the island known as Ka'iwi, same name as the channel to Moloka'i. The south shore is cranking today. But surfing will have to wait.

We skirt Hanauma Bay and descend the slope of Koko Head into Hawai'i Kai. In the distance looms the faint profile of Diamond Head.

"Dr. Kitagawa's home is barely a mile from here," Marie says, "on Kalaniana'ole Highway near the bridge over the harbor entrance."

Just before we reach that bridge, she tells me to pull off. I stop in front of a stucco two-story home with a Spanish tile roof. Marie steps to an intercom at the gated driveway. I can't hear what she says, but in a matter of seconds the gate swings open and I drive in. One door of a three-car garage rises to a shiny new BMW and out steps a neatly dressed man of about fifty.

Dr. Kitagawa gives Marie a long hug. Kula prances up to them.

"He's a beauty," the doctor says. "Come in. All of you."

Kula heads for our host's swimming pool and we climb stairs to a travertine deck. Below we see the retriever sniffing greenery around the pool and occasionally lifting his leg. Beyond in the harbor lie Dr. Kitagawa's two boat slips. In one slip is a small sailboat. The other slip is empty.

We sit in deck chairs and he offers us drinks that we politely decline. Our conversation begins with the subject of Marie. She and the doctor talk about her time in Paris and the sad history of her family.

Suddenly we hear a splash down below. *Kula.* He's jumped in.

"He loves the water," I say.

"I'm glad somebody is using that pool," Dr. Kitagawa replies. "I certainly spend enough keeping it clean and warm."

As Kula continues to entertain himself in the water, we move onto the subject that brought us here. Dr. Kitagawa recalls when he once shared a practice with Marie's stepfather and alludes to their falling out after her mother's death. Before then, Dr. Grimes had carte blanche to use his partner's second boat slip and also his extra car, an aging BMW convertible.

"I was attending a medical conference in St. Louis on the weekend Beatrice died," Dr. Kitagawa remembers. "When I returned I noticed that my old BMW was parked on a different slant in the garage. You know how it is, you park your car again and again and you always park it the same way. Well, when I saw the convertible after my trip I was sure I hadn't parked myself."

"Your wife, maybe?"

"She came with me to St. Louis."

"And so you assumed Dr. Grimes parked it?"

"Nobody else had a key. And there was no evidence that the house had been broken into. Besides, Gordon had told me how he could navigate between Molokaʻi and Oʻahu at night. He had the latest navigation equipment in his boat and he could also aim for the Makapauʻu lighthouse, which can be seen from West End Molokaʻi on a clear night."

As Dr. Kitagawa speaks I'm thinking that he's got a potentially crucial piece of evidence possibly linking Grimes to his wife's death, or at minimum undercutting his alibi that he was on Molokaʻi when it happened. But it's like the other evidence I've gathered, so far—circumstantial. Not concrete enough to indict anyone for any crime.

"If only Dr. Grimes had left something behind," I say. "And if only you had found it."

Then Dr. Kitagawa says, "He did leave something behind."

"He did?"

"Yes, I found it only a few weeks ago when I was giving my old BMW a thorough cleaning before trading it in."

Marie and I look at one another. And I ask, "What did you find?"

"I'll get it." He rises and steps into the house, then disappears into what appears to be an upstairs bedroom.

While Dr. Kitagawa is away my phone rings. Caller ID says HPD. *Again.* No doubt Frank wants to know when I'm returning Kula. I send the call to voicemail.

"Here," the doctor says when he returns. He hands me what looks like a cash register receipt.

I look over the receipt. It's faded, but I can clearly see on the top: MOLOKAI BEACH HOTEL.

"It's from the bar at the hotel where Gordon usually stayed," Dr. Kitagawa says. "The date is the same night that Beatrice died."

I check. He's right.

"And if that weren't enough," he says, "the receipt contains the last four digits of a credit card number, which I assume is Gordon's."

"Did Dr. Grimes ever use your BMW convertible again after this weekend?" I ask.

"Never again," he says. "We had our falling out soon after—I won't go into that in front of Marie."

"So he could have left this receipt only on that weekend—on that night that Marie's mother died?"

"That's right."

"Why didn't you go to HPD?"

"Like I said, I found the receipt under the driver's seat only a few weeks ago. And I figured if the police had done a thorough investigation back then, they would have known that Gordon was on Oʻahu that night."

Marie looks pale, as if she's just seen a ghost. She clenches her fists. She's always believed her stepfather pushed her mother from the cliff. Now Marie must feel she has proof.

"May I have the receipt," I ask, "or a copy?"

"Sure." He departs again and returns with the photocopy of the receipt. I snap the original with my phone's camera. On the photocopy I have the doctor write today's date and sign his name and state that it was left in his BMW convertible by Dr. Grimes on the night Mrs. Ho died. I ask the doctor to keep the original in a safe place because we may need to provide it as evidence.

Dr. Kitagawa offers his full cooperation. And again admits he doesn't care much for his former partner.

ten

Before we return to Kailua I check my voicemail from Fernandez. He says to call him back immediately. More about Kula? I'd rather not bother now, with Marie waiting in the car, but I may need Frank's continued cooperation on this case.

Speaking of Kula, he's soaking wet from his swim. We pat his coat with a couple of towels supplied by Dr. Kitagawa and say our goodbyes.

Then I return Frank's call. We get the preliminaries out of the way and he says, "Kai, I got a call early this morning from a Lieutenant Monet of the Paris Police."

"Monet, like the painter?" I ask.

"Yes. In fact, Lieutenant Monet tells me her husband is a distant relation of the painter. She speaks good English too, does Lieutenant Monet."

"That's swell, Frank. Really swell."

"Kai, now tell me the truth. You're surprised I know about Monet, aren't you?"

"Whad'ya mean, Frank?"

"C'mon, Kai. I'm a local boy from Kalihi. And you're wondering, what would Frank Fernandez know about French art?"

"The thought never crossed my mind, Frank." Actually, the thought *did* cross my mind.

"Guess what Lieutenant Monet wanted to talk about?"

I have a sinking feeling. "No idea, Frank. Tell me?"

"You, Kai. She wanted to talk about you."

"No kidding?"

"How about you stop by my office later this afternoon? I'll fill you in."

"Sure, Frank, I can do that."

"I'll see you then. And bring the dog. It's time you returned him to Maile." He hangs up.

"What was that about?" Marie asks.

"What happened in Paris is catching up with us in Hawai'i. Your stepfather and I are on the list."

Marie is silent. But no sooner do we get rolling on Kalaniana'ole Highway than she asks me to pull over. I do on the first street that comes up, Portlock Road—the road that leads to her family's home.

"What's up?" I ask.

"Let's confront my stepfather now," she says. "It's clear he did it and it's time to make him pay."

"A little early for that," I say. "We can prove he came to O'ahu that night, although he claimed he didn't. But we can't prove he killed your mother. Yet."

"It's so obvious!" she interrupts me. "Why else would he come here secretly on the night she died? And we know what Detective Fernandez didn't know—my mother was planning to divorce him."

"It looks obvious to me too and that's what troubles me. Frank may not have been at his best, but he's no dummy."

Then she says, "I'm your client. You work for me now, not for my stepfather."

"That's true," I admit, although she didn't have to put it quite that way. Then I recall that Marie, as pleasant and congenial as she can be, is an heiress. Should I be surprised when she behaves like an heiress?

"I'm going to confront him," Marie insists. "And if you don't come with me, I'll confront him alone."

"We don't know how he might react. He could get violent."

"I took a self-defense course in Paris," she says. "Nicole and I. We learned how to take a man down."

Bad idea. But if I abandon Marie to her stepfather and he harms her I couldn't live with myself.

"Okay," I say. "Your stepfather wants to see me anyway. But you've got to promise you won't attempt your self-defense moves. I'll defend you, if it comes to that."

Marie says nothing.

"Agree?" I ask.

She slowly nods.

I send Dr. Grimes a text that I'm in the neighborhood and could drop by if he's available. I apologize that I have my dog with me.

I get a text back almost instantly: "The sooner the better. Dog OK."

Before I drive the few blocks to Marie's home, she says she's not going to come in with me, but hide in the car so her stepfather doesn't spook and let neither of us in. Once I'm inside she'll quietly use a side door that leads to her bedroom and will wait there until an opportune moment. She still has a key, she says.

I think to myself, *That bedroom can't be full of good memories for her.*

Marie ducks behind me in the back where my board usually rides. So it's just Kula and me in the front seat when I stop by the palm grove and gate that hides the oceanfront estate. I step out, speak into the intercom, and hear Dr. Grimes' silky smooth voice once again. He expresses surprise that I've arrived so quickly and then the gate slowly opens and I drive in.

After Kula waters Dr. Grimes' ferns, the man himself shows up at the door, in his Freudian full beard. Kula's tail stops wagging. He doesn't growl, but he doesn't approach the doctor either. Strange. Kula loves everyone. Everyone loves Kula. Well, except Blitz.

"Come in," the psychiatrist says, "both of you."

I gesture to the sunny retriever. "Thanks for letting me bring him. He's acclimating to a new home, I'm afraid." The minute these words leave my mouth I wish I hadn't said them. But it's too late.

Dr. Grimes seems uninterested in Kula. He says, "Took you a while to get back to me. But, then, maybe you were still in Paris?"

I nod. No point in trying to explain.

He leads Kula and me into the foyer. I glance back at my car. No sign of Marie. We pass into the spacious living room that looks out on distant Diamond Head. I notice again the doctor's limp. And then I see his mountain bike and scale model of his former speedboat, SEA YA LATER. These two objects of his affection remind me that he prides himself on being what he calls an *active man*. In light of Marie's revelations, the phrase takes on new meaning. The doctor is no doubt a molester. Is he also a murderer?

I sit on one of two couches on either side of his mango coffee table. The doctor sits across from me. Kula plants himself on a rug by my feet, remaining tense and alert. There's something about the man that unsettles him. I stroke the golden and try to calm him.

Dr. Grimes doesn't waste time. "The reason I called you is because I've been contacted by Honolulu Police about the death of my stepdaughter's boyfriend in Paris."

I hear the faint sound of my car's door being snapped shut. Marie must be making her move to her bedroom. The doctor doesn't notice, but Kula's body tightens even more as if he's tracking a bird.

"Apparently," Dr. Grimes keeps rolling, "Paris Police contacted Homicide Detective Fernandez and I got the call from him."

"Yes, sir." I don't mention I just got the same phone call from Fernandez myself. Or that I'm hearing more footsteps from somewhere behind him. And so is Kula.

"What was that?" He turns around.

I shrug when he turns back.

"Anyway," Dr. Grimes continues, "Detective Fernandez remembers me from his investigation of my wife's death. He and I had several conversations back then, but he quickly realized I had nothing to do with it since I was on Moloka'i at the time."

I nod to keep him going. I have no idea what I am going to tell him. And I have no idea when Marie will pop out. Or once she does what she will do.

"Fernandez wants to talk with me in person," Dr. Grimes continues. "But I want to talk with you first. Paris Police somehow found out I hired you to deliver that envelope to my stepdaughter and it apparently appears to them that I was actually trying to target her boyfriend. I wasn't. But I want to know how they got from you back to me."

I hear more footsteps. Kula's tail starts wagging. The doctor turns around again and sees what the retriever and I see: Marie approaching through a doorframe directly behind him.

Instantly she starts in on him.

eleven

"You killed my mother." Marie speaks in a surprisingly calm voice. "You killed Pierre. And you abused me."

The doctor looks up at his stepdaughter and doesn't skip a beat. "Are you here to accept my offer?"

I don't know what offer he's referring to, but Marie isn't biting.

"No," she replies, "I'm here to make you pay."

"I didn't kill anybody," the doctor replies, also eerily calm. "Not your mother. And not your lowlife French boyfriend." Dr. Grimes doesn't deny abusing Marie. He just lets that accusation hang in the air.

"My mother didn't slip from that cliff," Marie continues. "We know you piloted your boat from Moloka'i to Hawai'i Kai the night she died. And then you took Dr. Kitagawa's car. You drugged her, put her in her car, drove her to Makapu'u, and pushed her. You were already back on Moloka'i before she was found the next morning. You lied to the police about all of that. We have proof."

I'm sitting here listening to Marie's recital that goes well beyond what we can actually prove, Kula lying tensely at my feet, and I'm watching the doctor take it in and wondering how this will all end.

"You've got it wrong," the doctor responds.

"That's a lie," she replies. "Do you want to try to tell us you didn't come to O'ahu that night?"

"I'm telling you I didn't kill your mother," he says. "As hard as it may be for you to accept, Marie, your mother probably took her own life. She was depressed, she had suffered a number of losses, and she succumbed to her despair."

"She was about to divorce you," Marie responds. "I told her what you did to me. She didn't believe me at first. But then she finally confronted you. That's why she died."

"Ridiculous," he responds.

"You left something in Dr. Kitagawa's car the night my mother died." She looks directly into Grimes' eyes. "It proves you were on O'ahu. It proves you lied to HPD. And it proves you killed her."

"You have nothing," he says. "You're bluffing."

"She's not bluffing." I pull from my pocket the photocopy Dr. Kitagawa gave me and I hand it to Dr. Grimes. "It's a receipt from the Moloka'i Beach Hotel bar on the night your wife died. You left it in your partner's convertible when you used his boat slip."

He peers at the receipt and slowly shakes his head.

"Do you still deny it?" Marie asks.

"This doesn't change a thing," he says. "Your mother went to the cliffs that night to hold vigil above where your brother died. It was a ritual of hers. She built a shrine to him on the cliff. She usually held her vigils at sunset. But she went that night because it was nearly a full moon."

"A convenient story." Marie bristles.

"Come with me to Makapuʻu and I'll show you," the doctor says. "Then you might be more receptive to my offer."

"To the cliffs?" I ask.

He nods.

I glance at Marie. Her eyes roll, but then she gets a faraway look as if she's having a revelation. She says, "Okay."

"We'll follow you in my car," I reply to Dr. Grimes. "You can drive your own."

"Meet me in the driveway." The doctor limps into another room, I assume to get his wallet and keys.

We climb back into my car and wait. Kula hops in the front seat next to Marie and puts his head on her lap.

Before long one of the doctor's garage doors opens and out comes a black Jaguar. He drives past us to the gate, which slowly opens. We follow the Jag as the doctor turns left on Portlock Road, cruises past his neighbors' oceanfront mansions, and turns onto Kalanianaʻole Highway.

The highway climbs the slope of Koko Head, then crests the ridge above Hanauama Bay and skirts the craggy, arid coastline on the southern tip of the island. We pass the famed saltwater spout at Halona Blow Hole and the body-surfing mecca of Sandy Beach before climbing toward the lighthouse at Makapuʻu Point.

The Jaguar makes a sharp right into the lot at the head of the Makapuʻu Lighthouse Trail. I follow the doctor into the jammed lot and search for a place to park. Eventually I succeed and so does he. I put Kula on a leash, grab a water bottle I fortunately have in my car, and we regroup behind the doctor's Jag near the trailhead.

It's hot and dry. The sun is blazing down.

"Follow me up the trail," he says. "Before we reach the lighthouse we climb off the trail toward the ocean."

"I don't believe this," Marie says again. "This is not my mother. What are you up to?"

"Maybe you'll learn something about your mother," he replies.

We give the doctor a lead of ten yards and stay behind him. Kula tugs on the leash. He's excited about the hike.

The first section of trail ascends the western bank of the ridge and is totally exposed. But the incline is gentle. The trail is wide and paved and very public, so it's hard to imagine Beatrice Ho finding a quiet place to hold a vigil anywhere around it. More reason to distrust Dr. Grimes.

Just off the trail ahead a mongoose darts under a low *kiawe* bush. Kula sees the flash and tugs on the leash. He wants that mongoose.

"Easy, boy." I encourage him to keep walking straight ahead. All I need is to lose the retriever on these cliffs. I grip the leash with both hands.

I also keep a watchful eye on Dr. Grimes. His limp is even more pronounced on the trail. He's leaning heavily on his cane. I start to have doubts about him pushing his despondent wife, or any able-bodied person, from the cliffs. And if he drugged her at home, how would he get her up the trail?

Of course, this lighthouse trail may not be where he brought her. He could have parked anywhere along the cliff edge by the road and pushed her.

The hike he's leading us on may simply be an elaborate ruse. So I continue to keep my eyes on him. And on his stepdaughter.

twelve

About halfway up, the trail switches back and climbs the ocean side of the ridge toward the summit. It's clear enough today to see Moloka'i's West End across the channel the doctor crossed that night—though he's still not admitting it.

Soon we get our first glimpse of the historic lighthouse, whitewashed and red-roofed, on the cliff's edge. The doctor stops and turns toward us. His face is flushed and glazed with sweat.

"We leave the main trail here." He points to a steep path that angles down toward the lighthouse.

Kula's tongue is already dragging in this heat, so I say, "Just a minute." I pull out my bottle and pour water into my cupped hand. Kula laps up the water that doesn't slip between my fingers onto the ground.

The doctor puts his hands on his hips, looking impatient.

"Stay behind me," I tell Marie. "And keep your eyes on your feet. You should be okay."

"I can handle myself," she insists.

As we step off the trail, the view of Moloka'i across the channel grows crisper.

Dr. Grimes hobbles down the slope—the dark sea frighteningly far below—heading toward the lighthouse. Kula pulls on the leash. He's still excited. I turn back and see Marie shaking her head.

"I don't believe this," she says again, loud enough for the doctor to overhear.

"Let's wait and see," I whisper back.

Dr. Grimes seems to know where he's going. We follow him at a distance.

As we edge down the cliff, getting closer to the lighthouse, another mongoose darts across the path ahead. Kula doesn't see it. Good thing. The dog could pull me off my feet. And down the cliff into the surf I'd go.

We pass beneath the lighthouse. The cliff gets steeper. One false step and any one of us could tumble.

Dr. Grimes struggles on. He's a slow and unsteady hiker. After another twenty yards of twists and turns, he steps off the path. There is barely enough room for the three of us to stand, and an ominous view of the ocean far below.

He gestures to a small clearing. "This is the spot."

"Where's the shrine?" Marie scans the trail. Then to me, "I *told* you he was lying."

On the upslope side of the trail he removes what looks like a camouflage net. Under it, sure enough, is what looks like a makeshift shrine. It's been several years since Mrs. Ho died and the shrine is looking weathered and beaten. But some mementos remain.

"This is where she kept vigil," the doctor says. "And this is where she probably jumped."

Marie and I step forward, Kula leading the way, to get a closer look. The shrine is the roadside variety with a dusty photo of an adolescent boy in a waterproof frame, some dead flowers and plastic flowers, a miniature toy surfboard, and a few other knickknacks that look like they might have been meaningful to Marie's mother.

Kula sniffs the shrine. Marie stoops down and picks up something small and faintly gleaming. "That's my brother's high school ring," she says. "And a photo of him with my mom. And another with his girlfriend."

"I told you so," her stepfather says.

Marie approaches him angrily. "You killed her!"

I stand between the two of them. "Keep your distance," I tell Marie and peer down. The drop must be four hundred feet, easy.

Gazing at this craggy cliff from which Beatrice Ho may have plunged sends chills up my spine.

I turn to the doctor. "If you didn't kill your wife, why did you lie to HPD about coming to Oʻahu that night?"

"I did bring my boat to Oʻahu," he finally admits. "And I did borrow Kitagawa's car. But not to harm my wife in any way. I didn't even see her that night."

I hear rustling in the *kiawe* brush. Another mongoose? Kula snaps to attention.

"Then why didn't you tell Fernandez?"

If I told him the real reason I came, he would have suspected me even more."

"Another lie," Marie says angrily. "You killed her."

"I came to see someone else," he says.

"Who?" I ask.

Before he can answer Kula takes off after a flash across the trail. I grab for the golden's leash but it's already beyond my reach. I make quick eye contact with Marie who's standing close to Dr. Grimes. She gives me a nod that she's okay.

I rush after Kula. He finally stops and sniffs the spot where a mongoose was apparently last seen. I catch up to him and grab his leash.

"C'mon, boy," I say. "Maybe next time."

Before I can turn and hike back to the cliff-side shrine, Dr. Grimes lets out a shriek behind me and then I hear a little avalanche of pebbles and shards rolling down the cliff. When I pick my way with Kula back to the shrine, Marie is standing alone. She's shaking. The doctor is nowhere in sight.

"Where's your stepfather?" I ask her.

She points, her hand trembling, down the steep slope to the ocean. I gaze far below. At first I don't see him. Then I do. He's a mere speck in the rolling surf. He's floating. Face down.

"What happened?"

"He fell," she says

You mean he just tumbled down?"

"Not exactly. When your back was turned he came for me. I knew not to trust him."

"And?"

"I gave him an elbow to the side of his head. He keeled over and lost his balance."

"And then he fell?"

"Yes, that's how it happened." Then she says, "I know I promised you, but it was either him or me. And it wasn't going to be me this time."

I stand there not knowing what to think, much less what to say.

She reaches her trembling hand into her purse, pulls out a cigarette and lights it. "God, if I ever needed a smoke, it's now."

I gaze at her, speechless.

Then she says, "He killed my mother. He killed Pierre. And he molested me. He would have spent the rest of his life in prison. So maybe this isn't the worst thing that could have happened to him."

"Maybe," I say. And wish I felt more convinced.

thirteen

Friday, April 12. 8:25 a.m. I'm sitting across from Frank Fernandez in his office at HPD headquarters on Beretania Street. He's already interviewed Marie Ho. Now it's my turn.

I've never met with Frank this early in the morning. He's kind of a night person. But this is a special occasion. A dead man was found floating yesterday at the foot of the Makapuʻu cliffs. The dead man happens to be my former client and Marie's stepfather. We happened to be hiking with him on the cliffs when he plunged to his death. So naturally Frank wants to chat with both of us as soon as possible.

Frank looks not quite so upbeat as the last time I saw him. Considering he's marrying the pet detective, I'm surprised. His dark moods are nothing I want to deal with this morning.

"Okay, Kai." He peers at me with tired and brooding eyes. "I want to know what happened up there yesterday on the Makapuʻu cliffs. Marie has told me the same story over and over. Can you corroborate? Can you shed some light?"

"I wish I could, Frank," I say. "I was twenty yards away. My back was turned. I was chasing Kula who was chasing a mongoose."

"That's another thing we need to talk about, Kai." Frank gives me a stern look. "We've got to get that yellow dog back to Maile. She's beside herself. It's already affecting our relationship." He frowns.

"Sure, Frank." I try to mollify him, wondering if he spent last night on her couch. I know that couch well. "We can talk about Kula. Maybe after all this business with the late Dr. Grimes."

"Let's do that," he replies. I doubt he personally cares whether the dog returns or not. Frank just wants to keep his fiancée happy.

"Like I said, I saw nothing except the doctor floating in the ocean below."

"C'mon, Kai. We've known each other a long time. We haven't always agreed on everything, but I've always been straight with you. And I've always expected the same from you."

"Frank, I heard him shriek and I heard some rocks rolling down the slope. But by the time I turned around he was gone. And she was standing there alone."

"Any words pass between them?"

"Not that I heard."

"Wouldn't you think, Kai, if the two of them—Marie and her stepfather—had an argument there would have been some shouting, some name calling, some threats that you would have overheard?"

"She said he came for her, she felt threatened, and she gave him an elbow. Her stepfather might not have said anything. And she—based on her past experience with him—may have sprung into action without saying a word."

"Could be," Frank says, but he doesn't sound convinced.

"Did Marie tell you what happened when she was a teenager?"

"She did."

"Okay. Well, there you have it. The man harmed her before and she had every reason to suspect he would harm her again."

Frank scratches the stubble on his chin. "Funny thing," he says. "I looked up Marie Ho's birthday, February 29. She's a leap-year baby, you know. Guess who was born on exactly the same day? Aileen Wuornos—one of the most notorious female killers in the annals of American crime. All her victims were men *known* to her—if you get my drift."

"So?" Fernandez seems to be grasping at straws.

"Aileen had a background similar to Marie's: orphaned, sexually abused, and mad as hell about it."

"I doubt Aileen was an heiress," I say. "And I can't believe Marie had anything to do with the deaths of her two boyfriends. Directly, that is."

"What about the two boyfriends?" Frank's tired eyes open wide.

"It's not worth going into," I say. "I've been over that ground myself."

"Let's talk about them later. Right now I want to know what happened on the cliff yesterday."

"If I could help you, Frank, I would. I've told you everything I witnessed. I'm in the same boat you are—I can believe her story or not. But hers is the only story we have."

"That's about the size of it," he says. "Even if I wanted to charge her, I've got nothing to stand on. And could you imagine her telling a jury about her stepfather's abuse?"

"The prosecutor could try to exclude that information from the trial. Or include it and make it look like a motive for murder."

"Yeah, but Marie Ho has millions to buy the best defense attorneys in the country. They'd find a way to get her off. So we'd spend a lot of tax payers' money to try her and we'd lose."

"That's the way it looks to me too."

"Of course, with him gone she gets back the Ho family estate in Portlock," Frank says. "He was legally entitled to live there until the end of his life. Which came abruptly yesterday."

"I suppose that could be another motive," I reply, "in addition to the years of abuse."

Frank shrugs. "The man wasn't exactly an eagle scout. A psychiatrist abusing his own teenage stepdaughter?"

"No. He wasn't an eagle scout," I agree. "And I like him for murder too. Maybe two murders—one in Hawai'i, one in Paris."

"He was no doubt a molester," Frank says, "but he wasn't a murderer."

"No? Not here or in Paris?"

"I got another call from Lieutenant Monet."

"Monet, like the painter?" I smile.

"Yes, Kai. Monet like the painter." Frank doesn't smile back. "Anyway, Lieutenant Monet advised me that I could cease my investigation of Dr. Grimes and of you, by the way, because they have arrested and charged their prime suspect in the hit-and-run death of one Pierre Garneaux in Paris. The suspect's name is Gustave Beauchamp of Lyon, France. Lieutenant Monet tells me the evidence is iron clad."

"Iron clad?" I remember the story Pierre's sister Nicole told me about Beauchamp and his vendetta against her father that Beauchamp took out on Pierre. It seemed farfetched at the time, but apparently not. "So Dr. Grimes didn't hire me to find Pierre in order to have him killed?"

"Right," Frank says. "Grimes may have even had his stepdaughter's best interests at heart. Sometimes when we get older, we regret things we did in our past and try to make amends."

"It's hard to believe," I say.

"The two guys Beauchamp hired to kill Pierre were apparently already watching your French professor guide, hoping she would lead them to Marie and her boyfriend. Then you arrived and steered them to their target. Completely unawares, of course."

Frank may unfortunately be right. I remember that grey Citroën following me around Paris. Not hired by Dr. Grimes, but by Gustave Beauchamp. In any case, I guess I became their unwitting spotter.

"So Dr. Grimes is clear of the murder in Paris," I reply, "but what about the murder on the cliffs of Makapu'u?'

"It wasn't murder, like I told you in the beginning, Kai. It was an unattended death. She either fell or jumped."

"But you didn't know Dr. Grimes was on O'ahu the night his wife died. You didn't know she had asked him for a divorce, after Marie told her about Grimes's abuse."

"You're right," Frank grudgingly admits. "We didn't know those things at the time. But we came to the right conclusion anyway."

"Then how do you account for the doctor being on O'ahu that night when he claimed to be on Moloka'i?"

"Remember I told you about the Ho's former dog walker named Krystal who was at a Yes concert that night at Blaisdell Arena?"

"Yes, I remember. The British band."

"Right," he says. "I just spoke with Krystal this morning. She broke up with Grimes a while back after a second patient accused him of sexual assault. That second case is apparently still pending. Anyway, Krystal finally admitted that Grimes was with her the night Mrs. Ho died. Krystal explained that she and the doctor usually spent weekends together on Moloka'i."

"I knew that," I say.

Frank rolls on. "This particular weekend was not only the Yes concert but also Krystal's birthday. So Grimes snuck away from Moloka'i after dark and under almost a full moon and piloted his boat in calm conditions to Hawai'i Kai Harbor."

"To Dr. Kitagawa's extra boat slip," I add.

"Right. Grimes didn't arrive soon enough to make the concert. And I don't see him as a Yes groupie, anyway. He met Krystal later that night at the Kāhala Hotel. They spent the night together, she now claims, and he left her before dawn and took his boat back to Moloka'i. She says he didn't tell us back then because their relationship would look too much like a motive to want his wife dead."

"Grimes was about to tell me yesterday at Makapu'u," I explain. "He said he had come to O'ahu that night to see someone, but not his wife. Marie didn't believe him. But before he could tell us, Kula took off after that mongoose and that was the last I saw of the doctor. Well, I did see him again, in the surf below."

"Too bad he wasn't able to tell you."

"What about Davidson Loretta, Mrs. Ho's estate attorney? Could he have gone to the cliffs and pushed her?"

"No chance," Frank says. "I spoke with Loretta again after our lunch at The Wharf. I was curious. Turns out, he now admits he was entertaining a lady in his room all night at the Halekūlani."

"A lady?" I ask.

"Yes, a lady not his wife. That's why Loretta put his male friend up to providing the alibi. Bottom line: There's no way Loretta goes to the cliffs of Makapuʻu that night."

"How much time would Dr. Grimes have served if Marie brought abuse charges?"

"That's not my department," Frank says. "At minimum he would become a registered sex offender, which might ruin his practice. But it's hard to say."

"You were right about Mrs. Ho's death," I say.

"That's not what her daughter wants to hear. But we still have no reason to suspect foul play."

I shake my head.

"None of us are right all the time," Frank says. "Not even me."

"Not even you," I echo his words.

"By the way, would you make sure Marie sticks around? I doubt we will charge her, but I don't want her leaving the island until we finish our investigation."

"Sure," I say. "I wish you and Maile the best."

He frowns. "Now about that dog—"

"Give me the weekend, would you, Frank? I've got a lot to think about. Plus Kula and I are going to hit the waves."

"Okay, Kai," he says. "But Monday I want that dog back."

I rise. "So long, Frank."

fourteen

On Saturday, April 13, I take the day off. I drop by Vivienne's home in Kailua in the afternoon, visit with Marie, and then take Kula surfing. Afterward I return him and remind her not to leave the island until Fernandez gives the okay. Then I spend the evening at the Waikīkī Edgewater.

Later that night I receive a voicemail from the pet detective. It may seem callous, but I don't listen. I know the subject: Kula. And I've told her already, I'm going to keep him as long as she keeps Blitz. Once she gets used to the idea, I'm more than willing to let her visit Kula. Without Blitz.

The weekend goes by and first thing on Monday, April 15, I head into Chinatown. I say good morning to Mrs. Fujiyama, who stands in her customary spot by the cash register, and climb the stairs to the second floor. I part Madame Zenobia's psychedelic bead curtains and peer into the incense haze. Shirley sits in her wicker throne—flaming red hair, thick mascara, beads and bangles jangling—hovering over her crystal ball.

"Here's your postcard from nowhere." I hand her the Eiffel Tower card. "Your crystal was right," I admit. "I did take a long journey."

"How about another fortune, Kai?" She moves her hands over the glinting orb. "On the house."

"No time," I say, my eyes smarting from the incense. "I've got taxes to mail off by the end of the day."

I slip into my office. As I try to massage the numbers on my returns, my mind wanders back to the cliffs of Makapuʻu. Frank Fernandez had been right. Beatrice Ho did, in fact, slip or jump. She wasn't pushed by her second husband, or by anyone else.

Fernandez' investigation had been flawed—he wasn't at his best—but his conclusions were as correct as we are likely to get. I was able to prove that Dr. Grimes brought his boat from Molokaʻi to Oʻahu on the night his wife died and borrowed his partner's car, both of which Fernandez entirely missed. The doctor's movements on that evening provided strong circumstantial evidence, along with a presumed motive, that he killed his wife.

Had I interviewed his former girlfriend, Krystal, I might have discovered, as Frank belatedly did, that Grimes made the trip to spend the evening with her on her birthday. In my defense, my client insisted I investigate her stepfather only.

My phone chimes.

A text from my client. Marie says she's on an airliner being pushed back from the gate at Honolulu International Airport. "Pierre's service is this week in Paris. Wouldn't miss it for the world. Aloha, Marie."

"Did you tell Fernandez you're leaving the island?" I text back.

"No time for that," she replies.

"What about Kula?"

"I hugged him before I left," she responds. "Key to Vivienne's house under doormat."

Before I can reply comes this: "Gotta go. We're taxiing to the runway."

That's the last I hear from her.

I scoop up all my tax forms, get my car, and head over the Pali Highway to Kailua. I pull into the driveway of Vivienne's home to the gregarious bark of the golden retriever. I step onto the front *lānai* and find the house key under the mat. I barely open the door and Kula bursts upon me—barking, wagging, his feathers aglow.

"Hey boy!" I wrap my arms around him and bury my face in his sunny coat. "I'm here for you."

I raise my eyes and see the kitchen waste basket tipped on its side and rubbish scattered across the floor. Not like Kula. I investigate. Quickly I understand.

An empty Spam *musubi* wrapper tells the story. Kula was hungry.

Marie had given him a taste of her *musubi* on the day her stepfather died. So how can I blame the retriever?

Picking up the *musubi* wrapper and assorted garbage I find an envelope. It's damp and stained, but the handwriting on the front is clear. *Marie*.

The same envelope I delivered to her in Paris that she said she promptly discarded? I look more closely.

Yes, the same.

I recall Dr. Grimes telling me the contents were for Marie's eyes only. But the doctor is now dead under suspicious circumstances and his stepdaughter Marie, at whose hands he died, has lied to me. I feel no qualms now.

I open the envelope and remove what appears to be three or four folded sheets and a return envelope, with international postage affixed, addressed to Dr. Grimes. The first sheet is a letter from the doctor to his stepdaughter:

Dear Marie,

I have tried to get in touch with you in Paris in every way I know how, but failed. So now I resort to having this letter delivered to you by hand. I would ask you to set aside your past feelings for me, whatever they may be, and to consider carefully what I am about to propose.

You no doubt recall that as a stipulation of your mother's will I was granted the right to occupy your family home for the rest of my life, the only benefit I received when she died. I am willing to waive that right so you can return and reclaim the home for yourself. The enclosed document sets forth the terms and conditions, and the consideration I would ask from you in return. I expect you will find the arrangement fair and equitable, and that it puts no strain on your considerable wealth.

Please sign and return the document in the enclosed envelope and instruct your bankers to render the sum to me.

Papa Gordon

As I'm reading this I'm wondering what sum Grimes is asking of his stepdaughter to reclaim her home. I thumb through the three-page document, which to me looks like legal boilerplate, until I come to the nub. *Five hundred thousand dollars.* Plus Marie must sign away her right to discuss publically details of this agreement and of her relationship with her stepfather. A gag order, in other words. Marie gets the house back, but it costs her a half million and also the right to expose his abuse.

And I ask myself why a medical doctor, a successful psychiatrist who conceivably makes lots of money, would give up living in such a beautiful oceanfront estate. Even for five hundred thousand bucks? The obvious answer: he needed money.

Then I remember Fernandez mentioning the recent sexual assault allegation against Dr. Grimes by one of his patients, not the first time in his career. I can only imagine that the cash the doctor suddenly needed enough to compel him to vacate the lavish seaside home had to do with that allegation and that patient. Either a pending suit or maybe even blackmail. And that also could be why he sold his beloved speedboat, SEA YA LATER.

The letter and document supply another motive for the doctor's murder. Instead of paying a half million to regain possession of her family home, Marie gets it for free. Not to mention revenge for his abusing her. I wonder again if the saying "the fruit doesn't fall far from the tree" applies to stepchildren.

"For Marie's eyes only" is now out the window. It's time to put this evidence before the eyes of Frank Fernandez.

fifteen

A few weeks later, on Monday, April 29, I'm driving through Waikīkī and see a couple of small sets rolling in. Hardly epic. But that keeps the crowds down.

I put my board in the water and paddle out to Pops, offshore from the Sheraton. The waves are only waist high. But conditions are clean and the right-breaking curls are sweeping all the way to the Royal Hawaiian. Before long I'm tucking into one of these turquoise curls and riding for what feels like forever.

On the long return paddle to the lineup my mind drifts back again to my unlikely case in Paris and its aftermath.

Marie Ho has not yet returned from Paris, despite repeated requests by Frank Fernandez. Marie claims that the late Pierre Garneaux's memorial service has been delayed for various reasons, but once it occurs she will come back to Honolulu. Frank gave up grousing to me about her when I announced that the heiress was no longer my client.

After I explained to Marie on a rather difficult long distance phone call that I found the envelope from her stepfather and turned it over to Fernandez, she refused to pay me. Bad move not to take those euros when she offered them. Then I told her if charges were brought there was only a slim chance, giving the lack of witnesses, she would be convicted.

"Convicted for what—a crime I didn't commit?" she replied. "And don't forget my stepfather killed my mother and he killed Pierre."

"He didn't," I said. "Not either one. You must know that by now."

She hung up.

After that phone call I began to wonder if there was any justice—moral or otherwise—in Dr. Grimes' traumatic end. He had allegedly molested his stepdaughter, cheated on his wife, and sexually assaulted more than one of his own patients. He was no doubt a despicable man, as my former client contended. But did his being despicable justify his death?

Frank Fernandez hasn't let a potential murder case get in the way of his wedding plans. He and the pet detective were married in a small ceremony only days after the heiress's surprise departure. I wasn't invited, but didn't expect to be. Since then Maile and I have arranged for her to visit Kula regularly—without Blitz.

Kula, meanwhile, couldn't be happier in his new home— Vivienne's home. I'm enjoying camping out with him until Viv's return on the first of May. We'll make an odd couple—a French professor and a surfer PI. Time will tell.

Back in the lineup I see a set rolling in. I paddle into position for the first wave, then watch another surfer take it. I let the next wave go by too. The third is the one I want. Glassy and almost chest high. And all mine.

I take off, tuck into this turquoise dream, and ride clear to the Royal Hawaiian.

Driving later to Chinatown, still stoked from my session, a kind of darkness suddenly descends on me. I can't seem to shake it. The darkness follows me to my office above the *lei* shop. I'm just about to put my finger on it when my phone rings. Caller ID says, TOMMY WOO.

I pick up.

Before I can say hello my attorney friend says, "Hey, Kai, did you hear the one about the Paris can-can dancers?"

"Can it, Tommy," I shoot back. "I'm in no mood for jokes about Paris."

He's uncharacteristically quiet. Then he says, "What's the problem, Kai?"

"The Paris case," I explain. "Actually, what happened afterwards."

"I'm listening," Tommy says.

This is rare. I better talk while I can. "I think I was a witness to murder."

"You *think* you were a witness to murder?"

"Well, I didn't see it exactly. That's the problem." I fill him in. Tommy has already heard about Dr. Grimes's fall. But he knows little about Marie's connection to it. And mine.

"What makes you think she did it?" Tommy asks.

"She had the motive and the means and the opportunity. She told me all along he deserved to die. Trouble is, I had no idea she herself would do the deed. If I did her stepfather might still be alive."

"Why don't you stop kicking yourself and let law enforcement take it from here?"

"I'm kicking myself because I'm the only person who could ID her. But I can't since I stepped away when it happened." I explain about chasing Kula who was chasing a mongoose. "That was her opportunity. And she took it."

"You didn't see a thing?"

"No. When I came back he was gone."

"What does Marie say?"

"She says she was defending herself. And Fernandez will be hard pressed to prove otherwise."

"You think she's lying?"

"She lied to me. Why not lie to Fernandez too?"

Tommy is quiet again. "So how can I help, Kai?"

"I don't know, Tommy." I give it a quick think. "What about justice? Will Marie ever pay for what she did?"

"If the law doesn't get her," he says, "maybe her own conscience will."

"Not if she thinks he deserved it."

"She can try to go on as if nothing has happened but, believe me, her old familiar and comfortable places won't be the same."

"She's got enough money to leave her old life behind— and go anywhere in the world."

"But she'd be living in exile," Tommy says.

"Yeah, I suppose."

"You're still kicking yourself," Tommy says. "What do you think you could you have done differently?"

"That's easy: Not go along with a client's demands that run counter to my best judgement. But it's tough when the client is an heiress who has just treated you to a first-class flight from Paris."

"We all face temptations," Tommy says. "You can be forgiven."

"Still I wonder, will justice ever be served?"

"Justice?" Tommy says. "Let me leave you with a good one: 'In the Halls of Justice'—said the late-great Lenny Bruce—'the only justice is in the halls.'"

I'm not as cynical as Tommy, but don't say so.

"Now stop kicking yourself, Kai." Tommy hangs up.

The dial tone buzzes in my ear and I set down the phone. While I'm grateful for Tommy's absolution, I know I could have done better.

Next time I'll be less reluctant to say no.

About the Author

Chip Hughes taught American literature, film, writing, and popular fiction for nearly three decades at the University of Hawai'i at Mānoa. His non-fiction publications include two books on John Steinbeck.

An active member of the Private Eye Writers of America, Chip launched the Surfing Detective mystery series with *Murder on Moloka'i* (2004) and *Wipeout!* (2007), published by Island Heritage. The series is now published exclusively by Slate Ridge Press. Other volumes include *Kula* (2011), *Murder at Volcano House* (2014), *Surfing Detective Double Feature, Vols. 1 & 2* (2017), and *Hanging Ten in Paris Trilogy* (2017).

Chip and his wife split their time between homes in Hawai'i and upstate New York.

Made in the USA
San Bernardino, CA
19 February 2020

64650435R00164